mooltiki

STORIES AND POEMS FROM INDIA

mooltiki

STORIES AND POEMS
FROM INDIA

BY RUMER GODDEN

1957 · NEW YORK · THE VIKING PRESS

DECORATIONS BY SHEILA AUDEN

PUBLISHED IN 1957 BY
THE VIKING PRESS, INC.
625 MADISON AVENUE, NEW YORK 22, N. Y.

Grateful acknowledgment is made to *The New Yorker,* which published "The Oyster," to *Harper's Magazine* for "Sister Malone and the Obstinate Man," to *Collier's* for "The Red Doe," and to *The Virginia Quarterly Review* for "Mooltiki," which appeared under the title "Elephants and Orphans."

LIBRARY OF CONGRESS CATALOG CARD NUMBER: 57-13052

SET IN WALBAUM, FAIRFIELD, AND LIBRA TYPES AND
PRINTED IN U.S.A. BY THE AMERICAN BOOK–STRATFORD PRESS

Contents

Contents

vi

I

BENGAL

Bengal River

Nothing can mollify the sky,
the river knows
only its weight and solitude, and heat, sun-tempered
    cold,
and emptiness and birds : a boat : trees, fine white sand,
and deltas of cool mud : porpoises : crocodiles :
and rafts of floating hyacinth : pools and water-whirls
and, nurtured in blue mussel shells, the sunset river
    pearls.

The boat hovers over the mussel beds,
and for these the divers go
naked into the water to work with nets and naked
    hands.
Split open the shell, the pearl is another world
evolved, revolved from a grit, and here, where the sky
    is vast,
the ball of the planet turns, flat below space, finite,

and is lost in the infinite worlds of the infinite stars
    of the night.

Here in the river is life,
life in the diver and pearl,
life in the wings of the bird, in the boat that is painted
    with eyes,
in the porpoises, joyously turning, wet and blue in the
    sun,
and the river is Ganges water with a ritual life of its
    own;
along its curious serrated banks in the grasses grow
    pygmy trees
flowered by mimosa balls that honey the hot breeze.

This, its indigenous life,
but there it ends;
there is no generosity in the sky, in the abstract tiger
    land;
the finality of the pearl, the gentleness of the flowers,
are evenly swept away; the boat of itself floats down
till the nets are lifted and gone and the fangs of the
    night come again,
and the little influence of daylight is lost along the
    plain.

Possession

The ricefield lay farthest from the village, nearest to the road. On all sides the plain unrolled in the sun with a pattern of white clouds, white pampas grass in autumn and white paddy birds, and glimpses of sky-reflecting water from the *jheels* or shallow pools. The sky met the horizon evenly all the way round in the flatness of the plain, an immense weight of sky above the little field; but the old peasant Dhandu did not look at the sky, he looked at his field; he did not know that it was little; to him it was the whole world. He would take his small son Narayan by the wrist and walk with him and say, "The field belonged to my grandfather and your great-grandfather; to my father and your grandfather; it is mine, it will be yours."

"I shall be a ferryman when I grow up," said little Narayan to his mother, Phalani. "I shall be a postman, and bring you a letter every day,"—but after he went to the fair at Pasanaghar he wanted to be a sweet-seller. He would cry, "*Jelepis, sandesh,*" and show his tray. His tray was a leaf fallen down from the palm trees and the *jelepis* were rolled of clay and water, but his father took it seriously and said, "No, son, you will be a cultivator like me and we shall work the field."

Narayan would nod his head with the sweat from playing still wet on his forehead and neck; then he wavered. "I should like so much to drive a bus, Father."

"You will be a cultivator."

The pampas grass waved its plumes in autumn; in spring the hyacinth weeds in the water opened spiked flowers of fresh mauve, and the honey-scented balls of the thorn tree sent their sweetness down the path that led from the village through the ricefields to the road. After the rains the path baked slowly to a hard clay whiteness, smoothed by the passing and repassing of naked feet; it was on its smoothness that Narayan had learned to run with nothing to trip him and make him fall. In those days Phalani made him a short coat of red cloth and tied strings with bells round his ankles, touched his eyes with kohl and oiled his sturdy back and thighs; he had been more beautiful and well grown than any little boy in the village. The anklet bells had tinkled as he ran, and the workers among the rice shoots raised their heads to look; Phalani's heart had swelled with pride and she smiled. Phalani's smile was like a water spring, it seemed to well up from deep in her and to flood her face and lips and eyes; she could only smile when she was proud and glad; she had no false smiles.

That was a long time ago in the village, but to Phalani it was now; if it was spring and the honey-scented balls bloomed, it was the same spring; the pampas grass waved, it was the same autumn; each year brought the same winter, the same heat and the same rains. Coming from the hut, carrying a bowl of curd or a *pân* leaf to Dhandu on his day-bed, she would look down the empty path. "I want to be a ferryman when I grow up. . . . I will bring you a letter every day." "You will be a cultivator. Your grandfather . . . your father . . ." But Narayan had been a soldier and gone to the war.

"War. What is this war?" No one in the village knew what the war was, though the schoolmaster and the post-office clerk from Pasanaghar read the newspapers. To the villagers, Narayan and the young men from the villages round who had been recruited were, simply, gone. "When will they come back?" the women asked. "When will they come back?" The schoolmaster and the post-office clerk shrugged their shoulders.

"But what *is* war?"

"War is like locusts," said the post-office clerk sententiously. "Like a plague of locusts devouring . . ."

"But—locusts leave nothing . . ."

The schoolmaster and the post-office clerk shrugged their shoulders again.

Phalani felt they should know more of the war than that; as the mother of a soldier, she knew war was not locusts. She was timid but she spoke. "In war," she said, "they have guns. My son has a gun."

Guns. The only gun in the village was the great old blunderbuss with its single barrel as long as a *lathi* that they let off to scare the birds in the mango grove when the fruit was ripe. It did not scare the birds but once it killed a dog.

The mango grove belonged now to Rai Bijay Ram. Little by little, Bijay Ram had bought all the land in the village; now he was a big landowner; the only bit left in the village not his was Dhandu's field.

It was a beautiful field. Lying next the road, it benefited by the slight incline that had come from the digging for water channels; the silt from the other fields washed down into it, and the silt was rich and the crop on Dhandu's field was always the best. Bijay Ram, Dhandu knew, would have given a great deal to buy the field and complete his ownership, but Dhandu's field was not for sale.

When it was warm in spring and in the hot summer evenings, Dhandu went down and sat beside his field, though the land was beautiful to him in any season: after the first planting out of the young shoots

when all the fields showed a tender green; when the
rice was grown and ready and the breeze made wind
patterns paler and darker as the blades bent and the
paddy birds waded like small cranes in the water; at
the beginning of winter when the rains had dried and
the earth was ploughed and the weeds were heaped in
small stacks in each field and set alight at dusk; then,
in the growing dark, the chequered lines of the small
fields were lost, the oxen were driven home and, one
after the other, the fires burned red and a spiral of
white smoke went up from each. It was all life to
Dhandu, and the health and strength of his land made
health and strength in his veins and bones. He gazed
at his crop and he felt secure; he had his land and he
had a son; only one son, it was true, but Narayan had
grown to a fine young man; with his army training
he had grown broad and strong, his muscles swelled
to hardness. His army pay was large; when Dhandu
thought of Narayan's English cigarettes, the excellent
leather of his belt and boots, the good wool of his khaki
greatcoat, he was weak with wonder. Dhandu had
never had a pair of shoes, only his village-made clogs
with a peg between the toes; all they had in the house
against the cold were quilts so old that the wadding had
come through the thin cotton cloth, and a shawl, a
chuddhar, that was cotton too; Dhandu's old bones
did not know what it was not to be chilled if the morning was chill, just as his stomach did not know what it

was not to be meagre. When Narayan laughingly put his army greatcoat on his father it seemed to Dhandu overwhelmingly warm and heavy. Narayan said he would send Dhandu an army vest; he did not send the vest but the very thought of Narayan in the greatcoat made Dhandu warm; the thought of his son was a warm, rich, safe tide of life.

When Phalani felt the greatcoat with her finger and thumb she smiled. No more than Dhandu could she understand how her son came to wear it, and she knew she could not understand. The first time Narayan had come back from school he had shown her the slate on which the schoolmaster had written characters for him to learn; Phalani had looked at the marks on the slate as if her soul would rake out their meaning, but it was no good; as fast as Narayan told her, she forgot. She could not remember I for INDUR from ì for ìGAL, not as much as Ā for ĀM or U for UT. "Mother, its *easy!* Even little Monmatha knows it!" Phalani could not, and she did not care. She had always gone to meet Narayan after school, she still felt the warmth of his little wrist as she had led him home; in all his growth she had felt his smallness, the babyhood that lies curled at the root of every man, while Dhandu had felt the manhood in the baby.

"Wait," said Dhandu. "One day he will come and work with me in the field."

When the telegram came that day the peon had

wanted money. Dhandu had some pice * in his waist
knot. "Give him one. Give him," Phalani had begged.
She had had a foolish idea that if the peon were given
money he might take the telegram away. "Give him
a pice," she begged but Dhandu said surlily, "I have
nothing for him."

"A *pice!* I want a rupee. It's a long ride to your
dirty village," called the peon, but Dhandu would not
give him anything and he had ridden away, his red
bicycle wobbling on the path as he looked back to shout
abuse. "Will a jackal's cry kill a buffalo?" said Dhandu,
but the telegram had been left. They had not known
what to do with it until the schoolmaster and the clerk
came running.

"Bad news," said the schoolmaster and had snatched
it. The clerk snatched it from the schoolmaster and
tore it open; the schoolmaster snatched it from the
clerk and finally it had come in two; by that time there
was a crowd, some of them on the schoolmaster's side
and some against him; it was not until later, in the
hubbub, that the schoolmaster had turned to Dhandu

---

* *The Indian money table:*

12 pies	1 pice
4 pice	1 anna (equivalent to 1 penny)
16 annas	1 rupee
100,000 rupees	1 lakh
100 lakhs	1 crore

11

and said, "I am sorry, very sorry, to have to inform you that Narayan your son is dead."

Dhandu had looked at them all making this noise in his courtyard. Suddenly he had taken up a stick and driven them out. "Get out! Get out of here! All of you and both of you," he said to the schoolmaster and the clerk. "Get out and never come back. Get out! Son of pigs! Get out!"

It was soon after that, or perhaps not soon, next summer or next spring, that Bijay Ram had come to see Dhandu.

At first in the village it had seemed that Phalani was the most changed. It was true that Dhandu seemed to have grown old in the night; that he had no more strength in his legs and could only totter from the hut to his day-bed in the courtyard, but his face, his voice, his look were the same, while there began to be whispers about Phalani. She did her work in the hut and the courtyard and field, she tended Dhandu, but it was a husk of Phalani, a body without light, without a smile; it was not Phalani because Phalani was not there. "She will go mad," said the whispers. "She is mad." Then one day Sukhdevi, the village midwife, had come into the hut and without a word put down in the corner a tiny string bed with a rag for a quilt and a homemade mosquito curtain bordered with tinsel. Round the bed Sukhdevi arranged dolls' cooking-pots, and platters made of clay, and in the bed a little clay

doll washed with white. "Krishan ji Maharaj has come
into your house," she said. "Mind you look after Him
well."

"Krishan!" whispered Phalani. *"Mother, I want to
be a ferryman when I grow up. . . . It's easy! Even
little Monmatha . . . Mother . . . I shall bring you a
letter every day."* The anklet bells tinkled on the path.
"Narayan Rajah. Krishan." Phalani put out her finger
and touched the image of the little god.

Bijay Ram came to see Dhandu. Dhandu, helpless
on the bed, greeted him with fierce pride. "It grieves
me to see your field," said the crocodile Bijay Ram.
"It grieves me."

Dhandu did not answer. He stared at a crack in the
courtyard earth through which a procession of black
ants was crawling. From inside the hut he could hear
Phalani singing, a soft little nasal lullaby chant, and
it seemed to him insane. Every moment of her day
was passed now in a ritual of worship in tending the
doll: for Him she kept the courtyard swept and washed,
the hut so clean that the earth floor shone; there was
fresh water in the pitchers, and the brass cups and
platters were scrubbed to gold; for Him she decorated
the steps and lintels with fresh patterns of white flour
paste, and brought in marigolds; for Him she gathered
dung and spread it on the wall in pats to dry for fuel,
for Him she ground millet and cooked; she cooked rice
and *chapattis* and a handful of vegetables until there

13

was no more rice, no vegetables. Soon she and Dhandu were living on thinner and thinner *chapattis* and water seasoned with pepper. Phalani's strength was failing; though her devotion shone in her eyes her body was wasting; she could no longer work in the fields, and the hoe and the basket stood idle against the wall.

"I grieve to see your field," said Bijay Ram.

Dhandu gazed at the ants as they filtered through the crack; in Dhandu himself a crack was widening and spreading. "Why not let my men work the field?" said Bijay softly. "That is better than letting it waste. We can share the crop, or, if you like, I shall pay you rent. You have nothing to live on," said Bijay still more softly. "A little money would be very acceptable."

Dhandu looked proudly at the ants but the crack was growing wider; his hunger gnawed inside him and from inside the hut came that weak singing.

"Why should anything be difficult?" murmured Bijay Ram. "We could arrange it as between friends . . ."

Dhandu raised his head. "Rai Bijay Ram Sahib," he said. "I am not your friend." Afterwards he was glad that he said that.

"*Ache bhai*," said Bijay Ram affably and went away. He soon came back. By that time Dhandu and Phalani were a great deal more hungry. Dhandu was so weak that he could hardly sit upright. "I have thought of something better," said Bijay Ram. He sat down by Dhandu. "I am your old friend and you do not trust me. I am deeply grieved." He sat looking down at his black patent city shoes with the black patent-leather bows and sighed. "I am deeply grieved." And he looked at Dhandu out of his small eyes. "I am so grieved that I have thought of something," said Bijay Ram. "To prove myself to you I have decided to lend you two hundred rupees."

"Two . . . hundred . . . ?" said Dhandu faintly.

"With it, as you do not trust me," said Bijay Ram with bitterness—but his little eyes twinkled—"you may get labour and work your field. Do not thank me," said Bijay Ram severely as Dhandu opened his mouth. "I do not wish to be thanked. You can repay me when you sell your crop, and I shall take surety from you."

"I have no surety to give," said Dhandu.

"Do not give your hut," said Bijay Ram. "That would be foolish. In case of want you must always keep your home; you can do it on the field. It is nothing," said Bijay Ram waving his plump hand and small gold ring. "You will redeem it, of course, when the crop comes; then you will pay me off; the interest for that time is small and the money will last a long time. You will not notice it," said Bijay Ram. "A pure formality."

"No," said Dhandu but he felt split with hunger and weakness.

"In a year you will have paid me off," said Bijay Ram, laughing gently. "You will not need more than a tenth part for labour and a little for your subsistence. You need not spend the rest . . ." But, without intention of spending, Dhandu spent the rest.

When he had put his mark on the paper Dhandu had been too hungry to feel a twinge; Bijay Ram had not advanced as much as an anna until the paper was signed; it was a fair paper with a fair interest but, as soon as Dhandu was comfortably filled, more comfortably than for years, he knew that he had betrayed his field. He put away the thought. "I shall get it back, *immediately*," said Dhandu. "I shall go to Bijay Ram and say . . ." He swelled as he thought of what he would say and how he would keep enough money back to pay Sharma, his neighbour's son, to work the field for the second crop, and a little back from that . . .

Once again the field was watered and planted and Dhandu was able, slowly, with his stick, to walk down the path and sit and watch the wind blow, dark and pale in the grown crop. He could see the crop was good. "And I have most of the money left," said Dhandu, "there in the hole in the wall by the bed."

There was so much money that he decided to repair the hut thatch and lime-wash the walls; Bijay Ram encouraged him. "And I should clean out the well," said Bijay Ram. "The crop will be good and you can afford it. How many," asked Bijay Ram, "have their own well? You should look after it. And mend the fence—or better, have a new fence. Sharma will do it for you with little expense. You can afford it. Why not do this?" asked Bijay Ram of one thing. "Why not do that?" of another. His eyes shone. It was he who suggested the warm shawls. "You are a land-owner," said Bijay Ram; "now you are old you should keep dignity."

"My father never had a warm shawl," said Dhandu. "He had a *chuddhar*."

"Your father never had two hundred rupees."

"That is true," said Dhandu. He bought a hen and a paraffin lamp; then he had to get a coop for the hen and buy oil for the lamp. Sharma needed a new basket. When the crop was harvested, and Dhandu and Phalani had taken what they needed, there was only a little left to be sold, and Sharma had to be paid; the second crop was poor and they ate it all. When the year was up Bijay Ram came.

"Well?" asked Bijay Ram.

"I cannot pay you."

"Then at least pay me my interest."

"Interest?" Dhandu lifted his head.

"Twenty rupees," said Bijay Ram. "You are lucky, the money-lender takes a hundred for every fifty." And he shook and chuckled as if that amused him.

When the twenty rupees were taken out of the hole in the wall there was only a rupee and some small

1 7

coins left. A year ago the two hundred rupees had seemed very large; now the twenty rupees seemed larger. "It is a lot of money," said Dhandu. He was reluctant to give it.

"It has been earned," said Bijay. His voice snapped like a crocodile's jaws—or was that Dhandu's imagination?

"You said you would pay me rent and now I pay you rent—for my own field," said Dhandu; he did not understand how that had come about.

At the end of the second year things were worse. There was nothing with which to pay Sharma, and the field lay uncultivated; shawls, lamp, hen all were gone and it was strange how the value changed from when something was bought to when it was sold. The old hunger came back, and worse, for Dhandu was trying to scrape this year's twenty rupees; he scraped and saved, but however empty their stomachs, the hole in the wall remained empty as well.

"And if I can't pay you?" asked Dhandu.

"You will owe me two hundred and twenty rupees," said Bijay Ram suavely. "Next year you will owe me two hundred and forty-two, the year after two hundred and sixty-six; in eight years it will have doubled, which is more than the price of your field."

Dhandu sat in his bed in the sun; he sat when Bijay Ram came, he preferred then to be upright, but the rest of the time, nowadays, Dhandu lay down. The sun reached him but did not warm him; a terrible chill was in his bones. Dhandu began to shake. Bijay Ram shrugged his shoulders and left.

Presently Phalani came through the courtyard from the path; she walked slowly, with great weakness, but she was smiling. She had been to bathe herself, and her hair, freshly washed, was coiled neatly; she had washed her old sari too and dried it in the wind, and she carried oleander flowers. She walked with a lilting step, and the sun fell on her shoulders and made her shadow clear as she walked. Dhandu raised his head. "Where are you going?"

"Inside." She showed him the flowers and smiled, looking towards the hut. "Then I must go to the bazaar," she said and broke off and smiled again. "There is a Nepali there, a trader. He has some little brass pots, real brass." She showed him the size with her fingers. "They are for children, but Krishan . . . Narayan . . ."

Dhandu's temper broke. Blindly he felt for his stick and tottered off the bed; he seized her by the shoulder and with angry strength he dragged her to the hut and up the patterned steps. "You are a fool! Fool!" he shouted. "Imbecile! Owl! Daughter of an owl! Narayan is dead. Dead!"

Inside the hut, in the gloom after the sun outside, he could see the saucer lamp, its wick burning in its earthenware bowl like a red spark before the little bed; no matter what they went without, Phalani found or begged the oil for this. The light shone on tinsel, flowers, cut-up fruit, grains of food. "Fool! Fool!" cried Dhandu. "Krishan! There is no Krishan. Narayan is dead. He is dead and we have lost the field. Narayan is dead." And he lifted his stick and brought it down on the lamp, smashing its clay. The lighted oil ran out in a puddle of fire on the floor; Dhandu jerked the bed into it with his stick and the fire ran up the curtains, which curled up and burned green as the flame caught the tinsel; the doll fell on its face, the food was scattered, and the clay pots fell on their sides or broke. Dhandu stood leaning on his stick, gasping. "Now do you understand?" said Dhandu. "They have killed my son. They have taken away my land."

Phalani did not answer; her fingers twitched, twitched, and her eyes never left his face.

There was the sound of voices and, from the path, two people came in and stood in the courtyard: a man in uniform and an Englishwoman. Dhandu hobbled to the doorway and looked glaringly down at them. Behind him Phalani went down on her knees and gathered up the broken pots.

"What do you want?" said Dhandu.

"We are the Indian Forces Families visitors," began the man. "Your son, Narayan . . ."

"I have no son Narayan."

The man looked at a card. "Narayan Chand. W.B.X. 13758."

20

From behind Dhandu in the hut Phalani began to sing, the same lullaby, but broken, sobbing.

"What is that?" asked the woman, and they pushed past Dhandu to see.

Phalani had put the doll back in the bed and was straightening the burned curtains. She did not know the visitors were there. "What is this?" the English-woman asked after a while.

"I think it must be the worship of Gopal, the Lord Krishna, in the shape of a child," said the man in uncertain English. "Very often it is made by childless women or those who have lost a child. They tend Him, look after Him. It has saved reason . . ."

"*Mother, its easy. Even Monmatha knows that . . . Krishan, Krishan ji Maharajah. Narayan. . . . Krishan . . .*" Phalani began to smile.

"She is quite happy," said the man. "She knows nothing at all." And, turning to Dhandu, he began to explain about the pension.

". . . . Accumulated pension and there is gratuity owing, in all more than two hundred rupees, and you will receive a further monthly sum. You see, your son still looks after you," said the man. "In this way he has not died. But you should have had it more than two years ago. You should have *applied*," said the man severely, and he said to the woman in English again, "These people are helpless. Helpless! What fate sends them, they accept."

When it was warm, in the spring, Dhandu hobbled down to sit beside his field. He saw it with its tender green, he would see it with the rice high, chased with its wind patterns; it would be harvested in the autumn, it would be ploughed, and weed fires would smoke in the evening. Dhandu did not look up at the sky or away to the great rim of the horizon; he looked at his field. Phalani, coming to fetch him, felt a small, warm wrist in her hand. "Krishan. New little pots, real brass."

She helped Dhandu to his feet and they stood side by side. They did not look at one another. Dhandu saw the field. Phalani saw her son. "It won't be a good crop. The rains were too early," Dhandu grumbled, but he smiled. He had his field.

"Mother . . . I want to be a ferryman . . ." Krishan. She had her son.

Sister Malone and the
Obstinate Man

Sister Malone had an extraordinary capacity for
faith. She was in charge of the Out-Patients in the
Elizabeth Scott Memorial Hospital for Women and
Children, run in this suburb of Calcutta by the Angli-
can order to which she belonged. She needed her faith.
Terrible things passed under her hands.

All sorts of patients came in all sorts of vehicles:
rickshaws, curtained or uncurtained; hired carriages
that had shutters to close them into boxes; a taxi with
an accident case lying on the floor so that its blood
should not soil the cushions, perhaps a case that the taxi
itself had run over—it was astonishing how often taxis
did run over patients. A few came pillion on a bicycle;
some could walk and some were carried; there were
fathers carrying children, mothers carrying children,
small children carrying smaller children. Sometimes

23

whole families brought one patient; servants of the rich brought their charges, or their mistress, or brought themselves. There were Hindu women in *purdah*, Mohammedan women in *burkas*, white coverings like tents that hid them from their heads to the ground, and hill women walking free as did the beggar women; there were high-caste, low-caste, untouchables; and all colours of skin, dark, brown, pale; and all sorts of flesh, soft, pampered, thin, withered, sweet, ill-treated.

There were diseased women, diseased children, burned children—very, very often, burned children; even more often there were tubercular children; deep and dreadful tubercular abscesses on breasts and groins and armpits were common. There was a great deal of ophthalmia and rickets and scabies, cases of leprosy and poisoning and fevers; and there were broken bones made septic by neglect or wounds treated with dung and oozing pus. There were bites from rabid dogs and sometimes bites from human beings and, like a repeated chorus, always, burns and tuberculosis. This was not the result of famine or of war, this was everyday, an everyday average in one of the departments of one of the hospitals in the city, an everyday sample of its pain and poverty and indifference and the misuse of its human beings. Sister Malone certainly needed that extraordinary faith.

The sisters who were detailed to help her always asked to be transferred after a few months; they became haunted and could not sleep, but Sister Malone had worked here for seven years. "*Sister*, how *can* you? I . . . You . . . I . . . I cannot bear it, Sister."

"You must have faith," said Sister Malone, and she quoted, as she had quoted a hundred, hundred times, " 'And now abideth faith, hope and charity, these three.' " She paused, looking through the thick lenses of her glasses that had the effect of making her look a little blind. "God forgive me for differing," said Sister Malone, "but you know, dear, the greatest to me is faith." Then a question, a little, persistent question, sometimes reared its head: was Sister Malone, then, lacking a little in charity, a little unsympathetic? Surely not. She was so splendid with the patients, though there was one small sign that no one noticed; the patients called her *Didi*—"Sister"; she spoke of them as "they," a race apart. "If only," she said—and she said this continually—"if only they could have a little faith for themselves!"

She tried to give it to them. In the corner of the treatment room there was a shelf on which lay paper-covered Gospels translated into Hindi, Bengali, Urdu, and Gurkhali. Sister Malone gave one to every patient. She walked sincerely in what she believed to be the footsteps of Christ. "It is seeing so much eye-trouble and lepers," said Sister Malone, "that makes it so very vivid. Of course Our Lord knew that lepers are not nearly as infectious as is commonly thought. People

25

are so mistaken about lepers," said Sister Malone earnestly. "I have always thought it a pity to use the word 'unclean.' I have known some quite clean lepers. Think of it, dear," she said wistfully, "He put out His hand and touched them and made them whole. So quick, and here it is such a slow, slow business. But of course," she said and sighed, "they need to have faith."

Sister Malone herself was a small, firm, flat woman. Her hands probably knew more of actual India, had probed it more deeply, than any politician's brain. These implements—yes, implements, because the dictionary definition of "implement" is "whatever may fill up or supply a want," and that was a good description of Sister Malone's hands—these implements were small and flat and firm; they needed to be firm.

At eight o'clock one blinding white-hot morning in June, just before the break of the rains, Sister Malone, Sister Shelley, and Sister Latch walked into the treatment room. Over their white habits and black girdles and the ebony crucifixes on their breasts they put on aprons; the crosses showed through the bibs. They turned up their sleeves and went across to the sink, where the tap ran perpetually, to scrub their hands, nails, wrists, and forearms, and afterwards immersed them in a basin of water and disinfectant.

Sister Shelley and Sister Latch were the two nuns detailed to help in the treatment room at that time. Sister Shelley was pale, her face drawn and sensitive between the bands of her coif; her eyes looked as if she had a headache. Sister Latch was newly out from home. Her steps were firm and certain; her pink face was made pinker by the heat; her body, well fed, solid, was already sweating through her clothes. She was cheerful and observant and sensible and interested. It was her first morning with the Out-Patients.

Through the window, as she scrubbed her hands, she noticed two little green parakeets tumbling in a gul-mohr tree. She would have liked to draw the other sisters' attention to them but she did not dare.

The Out-Patients was divided into the doctor's rooms, the waiting-hall, the dispensary, and the treatment room, which had a small examination room leading off it. The patients waited in the hall, which was furnished only by pictures; they sat in rows on the floor. They went to the doctor in turn and then, with their tickets in their hands, were admitted to the dispensary for free medicine, or to the treatment room for dressings, examination, slight operations, or emergency treatment. "You let no one in without a ticket," said Sister Malone to Sister Latch, "and you treat no one unless the ticket bears today's date and the doctor's signature. You can let the first two in."

Sister Latch went eagerly to the door. There was already a crowd and it pressed round the door, a collection of dark faces, clothes and rags and nakedness and smells. Sister Latch held up two fingers and cried,

"Two," in her new Bengali, but seven edged past her into the room. "It's all right," said Sister Shelley in her even, toneless voice. "There are only two. The others are relations"—and she set to work.

The first case was nothing remarkable, a septic ear; a woman of the sweeper caste sat herself down on a stool and, clasping her ankles until she was bent almost double, inclined her head to her shoulder so that Sister Shelley could conveniently clean her ear. Sister Malone was poulticing, in a woman's armpit, an abscess which had been opened the day before.

The next two patients came, and then another, an old woman. "You can attend to her," said Sister Shelley to Sister Latch. "She is an old case and knows what to do." Sister Latch went slowly up to the old woman. She was an old, underdressed crone, wound in a meagre grey-white cotton sari that showed her naked waist and withered, filthy breasts; her head was shaved and her feet were bare. She sat down on a stool and began to unwind an enormous, dirty bandage on her thumb.

"Don't do that," said Sister Latch. "Let me."

"*Nahin, baba,*" said the old woman, unwinding steadily, "you fetch the bowl for it to soak in."

Sister Latch had not been called "child" before. A little piqued, she looked round. "That is the bowl," said the old woman, pointing to a kidney-dish on the table. "The hot water is there, and there is the medicine." She had come to the last of the bandage and she

28

shut her eyes. "You can pull it off," she said. "It makes me sick."

Sister Latch pulled, and a tremor shook her that seemed to open a fissure, a crevasse from her knees through her stomach to her heart. The thumb was a stump, swollen, gangrened. "It—it makes me sick, too," said poor Sister Latch, and ran out.

When she came back the thumb was soaking and Sister Shelley was preparing the dressing. "She is a maidservant in a rich house," said Sister Shelley without emotion, "and they make her go on working, scouring cooking-pots and washing up; with the thumb continually in water, of course it cannot heal."

Sister Latch was dumb with indignation and pity.

At that moment Sister Malone came bustling back. "Ah, Tarala!" she said to the old woman in Bengali. "Well, how's your disgraceful thumb?" She took it gently from the bath. "Ah, it's better!" She examined it. "It *is* better. It actually is. Look, Sisters, do you see how it's beginning to slough off here? Isn't that wonderful? Give me the scissors. Now the dressing, Sister, quickly." Her fingers wound on the bandage swiftly and steadily. She finished and lifted the hand and put it in the bosom of the sari. "There, that's beautiful," she said, and the old woman crept out, still seared with pain but comforted.

"But *how* can it heal?" asked Sister Latch, with tears in her sympathetic eyes. "What is the use?"

"We must hope for the best," said Sister Malone. Sister Shelley was silent.

"We must temper our work with faith," said Sister Malone, emptying the kidney-dish. Through being steeped in ritual and reality, Sister Malone's words were often accidentally beautiful. "We must have faith for them, Sister Latch, dear. Sister Shelley, this child is for operation." She put a piece of brown paper under the child's dusty feet as he lay on the table. He began to scream as Sister Shelley took his hands.

The abscess on his forehead was like a rhinoceros horn; he was a dark little boy, and the skin round the abscess was stretched and strained with colours of olive-green and fig-purple. His eyes rolled with fright, showing the whites, and the muscles of his stomach were drawn in and tensed into the shape of a cave under his ribs. He screamed continually in short, shrill screams as the doctor came.

Suddenly Sister Shelley began to scream as well. She was holding the boy's hands out of the way while Sister Malone cleaned his forehead, and now she beat them on the table. "Stop that noise!" she screamed. "Stop that! Stop! Stop! Stop that noise!" Sister Malone knocked her hands away, spun her round by the shoulders and marched her outside, then came in quickly and shut the doors. "Take her place, Sister Latch," she said curtly. "The doctor is here."

"But—no anæsthetic?" asked Sister Latch.

"There's no money for anæsthetics for a small thing like this," said Sister Malone sadly. "Never mind," she added firmly. "It is over in a minute."

The morning went on growing steadily hotter, the smells steadily stronger, the light more blind and white. The heat in the treatment room was intense, and both sisters were wet, their hands clammy. In half an hour Sister Shelley, made curiously empty and blank by her tears, came back. Sister Malone said nothing. The patients came in until Sister Latch lost count of them; the wounds and the sores and disease and shame were shown and the room echoed with cries, screams, and tears—rivers of tears, thought Sister Latch.

Then, in the middle of the hubbub, quiet descended.

A car had driven up, a large car, and from it two young men had jumped down, calling for a stretcher. They were two well-dressed young Hindus in white, and between them they lifted from the car something small and fragile and very still, wrapped in vivid violet and green. Sister Latch saw a fall of long black hair.

The stretcher was brought straight into the treatment room, and the girl was lifted from it to the table. She lay inert, with the brilliant colours heaped round her. Her face was a pale oval turned up to the ceiling, her mouth white-brown, her nostrils wide as if they were stamped with fright, and her eyes open, glazed, the pupils enormous. Her hair hung to the floor and she was very young. "Seventeen?" asked Sister Latch aloud. "Or sixteen? How beautiful she is." She looked again and cried, "Sister, she is dead."

"She is breathing," said Sister Malone. Her flat little hand was spread on the girl's breast.

One of the young men was terribly unnerved. Sister Latch wondered if he were the husband. He shivered as he stood waiting by the table. "She t-took her l-life," he said involuntarily.

The other man, darker, stronger, said sternly, "Be quiet."

"And why? Why?" said Sister Malone's glasses, but her lips said evenly, "Well, she didn't succeed. She is breathing."

"You th-think th-there is—hope?"

"There is always hope," said Sister Malone, "while there is breath."

Then the doctor and orderlies came in with pails and the stomach-pump and the young men were sent out of the room. Sister Shelley went to the window and stood there with her back to everyone; Sister Malone, after a glance at her, let her stand. "You will have to help me," said Sister Malone to Sister Latch. "Be strong."

"But—only tell me what it is *about*. I don't understand," cried Sister Latch, quite out of herself. "I don't understand."

"She has poisoned herself," said Sister Malone. "Opium poisoning. Look at her eyes."

"But why?" cried Sister Latch again. "Why? She is so young. So beautiful. Why should she?"

"It—is best not to be too curious."

"Yes," said Sister Shelley suddenly, still with her back to them, "don't ask. Don't understand. Only try and drag her back—for more."

After a time the doctor paused; waited; bent; waited another minute; stood up and slowly, still carefully, began to withdraw the tube.

"No!" said Sister Malone, her hands still busy.

"Yes," said the doctor, and the last of the hideous tube came from the girl's mouth. He wiped her chin and gently closed her mouth and drew down her lids, but the mouth would not stay closed; it dropped open in an O that looked childish and dismayed, inadequate to the sternness of the oval of the face and sealed lids. "Snuffed out," said Sister Malone, as she stood up and gently put the draperies back and looked down on the girl's shut face. "They have nothing to sustain them," said Sister Malone, "nothing at all."

Sister Latch began to cry quietly. The young men came in and carried the girl away and, from the window, Sister Shelley and Sister Latch saw the car drive away, with a last sight of violet and green on the back seat. A tear slid down Sister Latch's cheek. "Forgive me," said Sister Latch, but no one answered; her tears slid unnoticed into that great river. "Forgive me," said Sister Latch, "she wore . . . exactly the same green . . . as those little parrots."

She stood in tears, Sister Shelley seemed chiselled in stone, but Sister Malone was tidying up the room for the next patients. "Nothing to sustain them," said Sister Malone, and sighed.

At the very end of the morning, when they had finished and taken off their aprons, an old man came into the waiting-hall from the doctor's room. He moved very slowly and led a small girl by the wrist; he held his ticket uncertainly between his finger and thumb as if he did not know what to do with it.

"Another!" said Sister Shelley. "It is too late."

"No," said Sister Malone with her faithful exactness. "It wants one minute to one o'clock, when we should stop." And she took the paper. "It is nothing," she said, "only stitches to be taken out of a cut on the child's lip. I remember her now. You may go, Sisters. It won't take me five minutes."

Sister Malone was left with the man and the child.

As she lifted the scissors from the sterilizer with the forceps she caught his gaze fixed on her and she saw that he was not old, only emaciated until his flesh had sunken in. His skin was a curious dead grey-brown.

"You are ill," said Sister Malone.

"I am ill," the man agreed, his voice calm.

Sister Malone turned the little girl to the light. The child began to whimper and the man to plead with her in a voice quite different from the one he had used when he had spoken of himself. "She will not hurt you. *Nahin. Nahin. Nahin.*"

"Of course I will not hurt you if you stand still," said Sister Malone to the child. "Hold her shoulders."

The child gave two cries as the stitches came out, but she did not move, though the tears ran out of her eyes and the sweat ran off the man. When it was over and he could release his hands, he staggered. Sister Malone thought he would have fallen if she had not caught him and helped him to a stool. His arm was burning.

"You have fever," said Sister Malone.

"I continually have fever," said the man.

"What is it you have?" asked Sister Malone.

"God knows," he answered, but as if he were satisfied, not wondering.

"You don't know? But you are very ill. Haven't you seen the doctor?"

"No."

"Then you must come with me at once," said Sister Malone energetically. "I will take you to the doctor."

"I do not need a doctor."

"But—how can we know what to do for you? How can you know?"

"I do not need to know."

"But you should have medicine—treatment."

He smiled. "I have my medicine."

His smile was so peculiarly calm that it made Sister

Malone pause. She looked at him silently, searchingly. He smiled again and opened the front of his shirt and showed her where, round his neck, hung a silver charm on a red thread of the sort she saw every day and all day long round the necks of men and women and children. He held it and turned his face upwards, and his eyes. "My medicine," he said, "God."

Sister Malone suddenly flushed. "That is absurd," she said. "You will die."

"If I die I am happy."

"But, man!" cried Sister Malone. "You mean you will give yourself up without a struggle?"

"Why should I struggle?"

"Come with me to the doctor."

"No."

"That's sheer senseless obstinacy," cried Sister Malone. "If you won't come, let me fetch him to you."

"No."

"Obstinate! Obstinate!" Her eyes behind her glasses looked bewildered and more than ever blind. Then they fell on the child. "You came for her," she said, "then why not for yourself?"

"She is too young to choose her path. I have chosen." There was a silence. "Come, Joya," he said gently, "greet the Sister Sahib and we shall go."

"Wait. Wait one minute. If you won't listen to me, let the doctor talk to you. He is wise and good. Let him talk to you."

She had barred his way and the man seemed to grow more dignified and a little stern. "Let me go," he said. "I have told you. I need nothing. I have everything. I have God."

Sister Malone, left alone, was furious as she washed her hands; her face was red and her glasses glittered. "Mumbo-jumbo!" she said furiously as she turned the tap off. "Mumbo-jumbo! Heavens! What an obstinate man!"

The Oyster

"To travel is to broaden the mind." Tooni, the sister-in-law of the young Indian student Gopal, had often told him that—but, thought Gopal, the mind can become so broad that it suddenly becomes a wild prairie in which it cannot hope to find its way.

"When in Rome do as the Romans do."

"To thine own self be true. . . ."

Which?

Tooni loved axioms; she had taught Gopal these, she had—"instilled them," murmured Gopal. Gopal earnestly intended to believe everything he was told, he knew that Tooni was sensible and wise, but now, suddenly, in this restaurant in Paris his mind had become a howling wilderness. "When in Rome . . ." "To thine own self . . ." Which? He was not old enough to see that by his travels and experiences he was taking the only possible first step to reconcile these conflicts, by beginning to find out what he was himself.

Gopal was sweet, naïve, young, almost breathless

with good will; yet he was dignified. René Desmoulins, the witty, dark French senior-year student, reading English at the university, had seen the dignity and especially marked Gopal out, though he was twenty-three to Gopal's nineteen. Everyone was kind to the young Indian. Gopal was charming to look at; his body was tall and slim and balanced, his teeth and eyes were beautiful, and his face was so quick and ingenuous that it showed every shade of feeling. They teased him about that but now he suddenly knew he was not as ingenuous as they, or he, had thought; he had come across something in himself that was stronger than his will or his desire to please. "Aaugh!" shuddered Gopal.

Up to this evening, which should have been the most delightful of all, everything had been delightful. "Delightful" was Gopal's new word. "London is delightful," he wrote home. "The college is delightful, Professor William Morgan is delightful and so is Mrs. Morgan and the little Morgans, but perhaps," he added with pain, for he had to admit that the Morgan children were rough and spoiled, "perhaps not *as* delightful if you see them for a very long time. . . . The hostel is delightful. . . . I find my work delightful." He had planned to write home that Paris was delightful. "We went to a famous French restaurant in the rue Perpignan," he had meant to write, "it is called the Chez Perpignan. It is de——" Now tears made his dark

eyes bright; he could not write that; it was not delightful at all.

Through his tears he seemed to see far beyond the
white starched tablecloth marked "Perpignan" in a
red cotton laundry mark, beyond the plates and glasses,
the exciting bottle of wine of which he had asked to
inspect the label after the waiter had shown it to René.
He saw beyond the single scarlet carnation in the vase
on the table, beyond everything in the restaurant that
had thrilled him as they came in; the dark brown walls
with their famous old theatre posters—"French printed
in French!" Gopal had exclaimed as if he had not
really believed that French could be printed—the serv-
ing table where a flame burned under a silver dish and
a smell rose into the air, mingling with other strange
and, to him, piquant smells, of hot china plates, starch,
coffee, toast, old wine-spills, food, and clothes. He saw,
beyond them all, the low tables spread for dinner at
home, one of the dinners that he had always thought
most ordinary, old-fashioned, and dull, prepared by
his mother and Tooni.

Gopal's family lived in Bengal; they were Brahmini
Hindus and his mother kept the household to orthodox
ways in spite of all he and his elder brother could do.
Now Gopal saw her orthodox food: the flat brass
platters of rice, the pile of *luchis*—flaky, puffed, pale
gold biscuits—the vegetable fritters fried crisp, the
great bowl of lentil purée, and the small accompanying

bowls of relishes—shredded coconut or fried onion or spinach or chilis in tomato sauce or chutney, all to be put on the rice. He saw fruit piled on banana leaves, the bowl of fresh curd, the milk or orange or bel-fruit juice in the silver drinking tumblers; no meat or fish, not even eggs, were eaten in that house. "We shall not take life," said his mother. Gopal looked down at his plate in the Perpignan and shuddered.

He had come to Europe with shining intentions, eager, anxious to do as the Romans did, as the English, the French, as Romans everywhere. "There will be things you will not be able to stomach," he had been warned; so far he had stomached everything. His elder brother Jai had been before him and had come back utterly accustomed to everything Western; when Jai and Tooni went out to dinner they had Western dishes; they ate meat, even beef, but not in their own home. "Not while I live," said his mother, and she had told Gopal, "You are not the same as Jai. You are not as coarse."

"Oh I am, Mother," Gopal had pleaded, "I am just as coarse." But now another shudder shook him.

"Are you cold, Gopal-ji?" asked René.

Gopal had taught René the endearment; he had thrilled to hear him use it, and even now he managed to smile, though in truth even his lips were cold. "I am not at all cold," lied Gopal. "This is—delightful."

If it had been the cold that upset him it would have

been nothing; all Indians were supposed to feel the cold. Gopal did not mind the lack of sun, the grey rain, though several Western things were very strange to him; the perpetual wearing of shoes, for instance, made his feet ache, but he had liked his feet to ache; he had been proud of them when they ached, he felt they were growing wise. Now he wriggled his toes in his shoes under the table and would have given anything to be sitting with bare, sun-warmed feet. A feeling that he had not had all his time abroad welled up in him; he felt sick, sick for home.

He saw his own family front door, with the family shoes dropped down in a row at the entrance; he saw the hall, empty of everything but a rickety hat rack that never had a hat hung on it—how could it? They wore no hats. He thought how he would come in, drop off his shoes on the step, and go to the tap to wash and take off his shirt, calling out to his mother and Tooni in a lordly way, "Isn't there anything to eat in this house?" His mother, who never knew a joke when she heard one, would begin to shoo the maidservant and Tooni about and hurry them, and presently Tooni would bring him a few sweets in a saucer to keep him quiet.

> *"O Soul, be patient, thou shalt find*
> *a little matter mend all this,"*

Tooni would say, and she would add, "That is by Robert Bridges. Bridges was once Poet Laureate of

England." Tooni was always anxious to improve her little brother-in-law.

In Europe, Gopal had eaten everything. "Roast lamb, kidneysontoast, baconandsausage," murmured Gopal, and when René, who, being a Frenchman, had a proper feeling for food, had talked of the food they would eat in Paris, Gopal had not flinched, though some of it sounded rather startling to him—"rather *bare*," he had written to Tooni. "Imagine sucking-pig, Tooni," he had written, "and René says it is laid out whole on the dish; *tête de veau*, and that is calf's head with its eyes and its brain all there. He says we shall have steak, *rare*, I don't know what that means but I shall find out, and oysters, I shall eat oysters. What are oysters? I shall find out. I shall come back more Parisian than Paris!"

René, the dazzling, elderly René, had asked Gopal home with him to Paris for the vacation. "It is a delightful *compliment*," Gopal wrote, "and, let me tell you, there are not many he would ask, but he asked me!"

René, with his brilliance, his terse, quick wit, his good looks, his ruthlessness and his foreignness, was venerated by the students and a little feared by the masters, which made him all the more popular and, when he was kind to Gopal, Gopal was completely dazzled. "You are too good to me," he gasped, and, shyly—"You must love me very much."

René had the grace not to laugh at him. "You do not know *how* delightful he is!" wrote Gopal to his mother, and to Tooni he wrote, "René is like Hamlet, only humorous; like Byron, only good." He looked at these two comparisons and their qualifications; they seemed to come out null and void, and he tried again. "He is like Jesus Christ," he wrote reverently, "only very, very sophisticated." For René, Gopal would have made one of those pilgrimages sometimes made by the devout in India, on which, at every step, the pilgrim measures his length in the dust.

On that thought, Gopal realized how much he missed the dust. What a funny thing to miss, he thought, but he missed the dust. He wriggled his toes uncomfortably in his shoes and thought he could even smell the dust of his own great Bengal town. It seemed to rise in his nostrils as he looked out of the restaurant window. Across the Paris twilight and its multitudinous lights, he seemed to see the small oil flares of the orange-sellers' booths on a certain narrow pavement near his home. He heard the car horns, not Paris horns but the continuous horns of the Sikh taxi-drivers; he heard bicycle-rickshaw bells, the shuffling feet and the pattering noise as a flock of goats was driven by. He wanted to go home, past the white oleander bushes by the gate, past the rows of shoes, up to his own small room where on moonlight nights the shadow of the fig tree and the bars of his barred window were thrown together on the whitewashed wall. How many nights had he lain on his bed and watched the shadow leaves move, stir gently in the heat, as he had wondered about going away far over the sea to travel in Europe, in England and, yes, in France? Now in France he thought, as he had never thought he could think, of that small room and the tears stung his eyes again.

René saw the tears and was concerned. Under the terseness and the sophistication René was simple and young and kind. "What is it, Gopal-ji?" he asked.

"I—swallowed—something hot," said Gopal.

"But you are used to hot things."

"Yes, chilis," said Gopal and laughed, but it was not safe to think of such homely things as chilis; they made him see a string of them, scarlet, in the kitchen. He saw the kitchen, and his mother's housekeeping, which had often seemed to him old-fashioned and superstitious, now seemed as simple and pure as a prayer; as—as uncruel, he thought. His mother rose at five and woke the children so that they could make their morning ritual to the sun; many and many a time had she gently pulled him, Gopal, sleepy and warm and lazy, from his bed. She saw that the house was cleaned, then did the accounts and then, still early, sent Jai, as the eldest son, to market with the list of household things to buy and the careful allowance of money—few Indian women shopped in the market. When Jai came back, with a coolie boy carrying the basket on his head, the basket had a load of vegetables, pale green lettuce and lady's-fingers, perhaps, or glossy, purple eggplants, beans, the pearly paleness of Indian corn still in its sheaf. There would be coconut too, ghee-butter, and the inevitable pot of curd made fresh that day.

The kitchen was very clean; no one was allowed to go there in shoes or in street clothes, and before Gopal and Jai ate they washed and changed or took off their shirts. The women ate apart, even the go-ahead Tooni. All was modesty, cleanliness, quiet—and it does no hurt, thought Gopal, shuddering. All of it had an inner meaning so that it was not—not just of earth, he thought. Once a month was household day when the pots and pans and sweeping brushes were worshipped. First they were cleaned, the brass scoured with wood-ash until it shone pale gold, the silver made bright, the brushes and dusting-cloths washed, cupboards turned out, everything washed again in running water and dried in the sun; then prayers were said for the household tools, and marigold flowers and jessamine were put on the shelves. I used to think it was stupid, thought Gopal; I teased my mother and called her ignorant to believe in such things, but they made it all different, quite different!

"Gopal, what *is* the matter?" asked René and he laid his hand on Gopal's.

In India it is usual for young men who are friends

to hold hands; for René to take Gopal's hand would have filled him with pride half an hour ago; now he flinched, and the intelligent René felt him flinch and took his own hand away and looked at Gopal closely. "Explain what it is," suggested René gently, but Gopal shook his head. He could not explain; how could he tell René that, for the first time, he saw not what the world did to Gopal but what he, Gopal, did to the world?

Last night he had found out what "rare" steak is; he had cut the meat red and eaten it, only thinking of the redness going into him and wondering if he could get it down, could "stomach" it; now, suddenly, everything was in reverse. René had ordered the famous oysters and Gopal had looked so doubtfully at the plate of grey-brown shells and the strange, glutinous, greenish objects in each, that René had laughed. "Pepper one, squeeze a little lemon on it, and let it slide down your throat," said René. He had shown Gopal and Gopal had copied him but, when Gopal squeezed the lemon juice on his oyster, he had seen the oyster shrink.

"But—but it's alive!!!"

"Of course it's alive. It would be dangerous to eat it otherwise. If they served you a dead oyster," René had said gravely, "I should have to take it out and show it to a policeman." Seeing Gopal's face, he said, "Don't worry; it will die as soon as it touches you."

"Auhaugh!" said Gopal.

René had laughed. Now, remembering that, Gopal seethed with rage. His ears were burning, his cheeks and his heart; the plate with the oysters seemed to swim in front of him. Centuries of civilization, of learning, of culture, to culminate in this!

"What *is* the matter?"

"You are a barbarian," said Gopal in a low, burning voice. He trembled to speak like this to René, but he spoke. "Your ancestors were running about in blue skins," said Gopal, "when mine had religion, a way of life." For a moment he stopped; René, in a blue skin, would look like Krishna; Krishna, the Hindu God, often had a blue skin, he played the flute and was the God of Love and had many amiable peccadilloes, but Gopal hardened his heart against René, even in his most lovable aspects. It was this learning, this culture, this barbarism, that he had come all this way to share. I want to go home, thought Gopal. I want to go home.

"You all think we Indians should study your customs, why don't you study ours?" he cried to René. "We could teach you a thing or two! Why should we have to Westernize? Why don't you Easternize? It would do you a lot of good, let me tell you that. You are cruel," cried Gopal. "You are not even honest. In England they teach children 'Little Lamb, who made thee?' and give them the roast lamb for lunch, lamb

with mint sauce. Yes! you eat lamb and little pigs and
birds. You are cruel. Cruel and barbarous and greedy
and—" He broke off, trying to think of the word he
wanted; it meant "too much." Ah, yes! a dozen dozen,
thought Gopal, and hurled the word at René. "You
are *gross!*" he cried, and stopped. Though he was sitting down, even his legs were trembling. The effort
had left him weak. "You are gross," he said in a
whisper.

"You are perfectly right," said René. He put another oyster down his throat, but there was something so mild, so tempered in his reply that Gopal
was checked.

"These are things," said René when he had finished the oyster, "that a man has to arrange for himself."

It was not only a small rebuke, it was a suggestion
made as Tooni would have made it, but of course
Tooni was not as subtle and delicate as René, the same
René who was now preparing to eat the last oyster on
his plate—and he had a dozen, thought Gopal, when
I had ordered only six! Subtle, delicate René, who was
gross and delicate, fastidious and greedy, ruthless and
mild. Gopal shook his head in despair.

"Travel broadens the mind." Then if it is broad,
thought Gopal, it has to include all sorts of things; he
looked at René's hand, putting pepper and squeezing
the lemon—that clever, cruel hand. The world, when

it was opened out, was not delightful; no, not delightful at all, thought Gopal. It had a bitter taste; he did not like it.

"When in Rome, do as the Romans do." René was a Roman of Romans; now, with grace and elegance, he slid the oyster down his throat and smiled at Gopal. René agreed that he was not delightful; he was content not to be—no, not content, thought Gopal, looking at him; he knows that he cannot hope to be, all of him, delightful. And if René can't, thought Gopal in despair, who can? Excepting— Well, it is easy if you stay in one place, in your mother's kitchen but— if you go into Rome?

He thought of that steak, *rare;* he had eaten it and now in his mind there was a vision of the sacred bull that came every day to their house to be fed; he saw its soft, confident nose, its noble face and the eyes lustrous with thick, soft eyelashes; its cream dewlap swung like a fold of heavy velvet and it wore a cap worked in blue and white beads on its hump; Gopal had saved up to buy that cap with his own money.

"To thine own self . . ." Tooni seemed very far away. Gopal turned away his head.

At that moment, René having beckoned, the waiter came and took the plate of oysters away.

"Now what shall we eat?" asked René and he asked, "Have you ever tasted *vol-au-vent?*"

"How strange! It sounds like hitting balls at tennis," said Gopal, beginning to revive.

"It isn't tennis, it's chicken," said René. "Would you like to try it?"

"Chicken?" The word seemed to hang in the balance; then Gopal asked, "Is it new? Is it exciting?"

"Well . . ." René could not say *vol-au-vent* was exciting. "You may like it."

"Nothing venture, nothing win," said Gopal, and René gave the order to the waiter.

"This is delightful," said Gopal.

II

HIMALAYAN
NOMADS

The Goat People:
Pastoral Poems

Every year in spring in the Himalayas of northern
India, the *Gujars*, shepherds, and the *Bakriwars*, liter-
ally "goat people," drive their flocks up from the
plains to summer in the high valley and plateau pastures in the mountains where they have left their huts.

In the Himalayas, the spring melts the snow into ice
streams in a wilderness of flowers, alpine, mountain,
wild, in the rich young grass. All April and early May
the flocks are driven along the roads in clouds of dust
—countless head of long-coated, long-horned goats;
great, slow-moving buffaloes; stringy ponies and fierce
dogs like close-coated Eskimo huskies.

These people are nomad, Mohammedan, though
they look Biblical and have Biblical names: Jassoof,
Ezekiel, Daveed. They live in small tribes or clans

and choose two or three among themselves as Elders, though the Elders may be quite young. On march, the men look after the flocks but do not carry anything unless it is a child or a kid.

The tribes pass all through the spring, pitching their camp at night and lighting their fires under a boulder or a fir tree, or by an ice stream; moving on again at dawn, driving with a peculiar trembling whistle that is their own, something between a hawk's cry and a flute, harsh, sweet, and wild.

They summer on the high Himalayan meadows that have beautiful Kashmiri names: Gulmarg, meadow of roses; Sonamarg, meadow of gold; Nilnag, blue lake; the Hill of Torrents and Bridges and Stones; the Cock's Chest; the Window of Gladness.

In the autumn the tribes move down again to winter in the vale of Kashmir or in Poonch on the plain.

I have tried to make these poems like the people, rough and rhythmical (in fact, in some of them, with a rhythm so marked that it may be called doggerel), without symbolism or image, simple and pastoral.

THE MEADOW

It is a blue meadow inverted to the sky
where eagles fly
in a ring
of mountains, towering,
and no wing,
in however thin and giddy circles flown,
can cut across a summit, a peak or soaring height,
the colour of slate pencils or of pumice stone
where the snow has gone.
There are perpetual fields of ice and glacier
and forests of dark fir
and woods of snow-distorted birch with silver bark
as pale as the fir leaves are dark.
Perpetually on the passes there is snow
unbroken, white,
leading to the plateaus where the shepherds go,
nomad tribes with herds of ponies, foals and goats
    and buffalo.

They have begun their upward journeying,
the caravans endlessly swing
by day and night
with ponies, herds, dogs, babies, tents, blankets, and
    cooking pots, far up and out of sight.

57

THE CARAVAN

A caravan:
at every pony's head a man.
Every pony with its load
strung,
one by one,
down the road.
It has met
other caravans from Tibet,
other ponies with other packs,
yaks
and zos with heavy tails
carrying bales
of yak wool on their backs.
The road goes
through the lush lower valley, while the pinnacle of
    snows
shuts off the sky
and, high,
its vision broken by that eagle's wing,
are upland meadows, forests, waterfalls
and green alps where larks sing.
The flocks go past with the herdsmen, bearded, Biblical;
    they make their camp near a Bible river of rushing
    crystal.
At night there is only the sound of the river, of the

fire and the cattle grazing as they move gently
  over the ground;
perhaps, all the way to Tibet tonight, there is no other
  sound.

FLOWERS FOR THE ANIMALS

In the meadow it is spring;
the sun warms and, from the softening snowfields, the
  avalanches fall and the rocky gorges thunder with
  their slips.
Crevasses open sudden hungry lips
as blue as a kingfisher's wing. The streams are spreading from the melting snow and in high lonely lakes,
sheer fathoms in the crater's cup, ice shivers and grinds
  and breaks.
Now, in every glacier crack, are primulas, speedwells,
  scyllas,
anemones, gentian, edelweiss, potentillas;
the meadow has red and white clover, an alp of lark-
  spur grows
by bushes of the prickly mountain rose.
There are blue poppies and geums, deep wild borage
and all the lesser flowers, brilliant, savage,
and lemon-scented thyme that has dark buds,
above, on eagle rocks, saxifrage and alpine flowers in
  wild cold solitudes.
All this goes into honey, milk, and cuds;

the flowers give their little balmy death
and every animal has a sweet-scented breath.

THE ELDERS

There is a flat rock among the huts below the birch
    trees
where the elders sit out on summer evenings and quar-
    rel,
smoke and talk about money and discuss
the affairs of the tribe; they sit, scratch comfortably
    for fleas.
The Patriarch has the beard of the Faithful dyed deep
    sorrel
and his turban glows the colour of an autumn crocus.

How much,
how much,
did it cost?
Did it pay?
Was it worth?

Ouch! Ouch!
Such and such
was lost
on the way
from the North.

Two pice
a seer
on the price
of rice!
Allah! What has come over the earth!

Advice
(given twice)
that young Jassoof should be married.
Jassoof . . .

Once we were young . . .
but the tribe is strong,
Shah's Bibi has given birth
at last to the son she carried.

The waterpipes gurgle peacefully, the light
leaves the valley and draws up the mountain to the
    snowpeaks and the sky, where it shines in sun and
    changes to the first stars of the night.
A boy comes out with salt tea and a handful of apricots
and the *samowar* presses a circle flat in the forget-
    me-nots.

How much
did it cost?
Did it pay?
Was it worth?

THE GOAT WOMEN

Their trousers are romantic, their swinging clothes
in black and damson red, crimson and smoke-stained
  rose,
and the bracelet cap, the colour of a hill jay's dark
  blue tail,
and, shadowing the oval of each face, a loose black veil.
They walk barefoot, their anklets chinking up the
  narrow, stoned track,
on their heads the cooking pots of the tribe, iron,
  netted in strings,
a sick hurt goat or kid at their heels and, downward-
  nodding from slings,
a dark-eyed baby on every nonchalant back.

To the men they are like cattle, desirable as stock,
even with horses and buffaloes, a prize foal or a fine
  goat flock,
given with the scarlet wedding clothes and the silver
  jewellery,
valued for spirit, endurance, beauty, and reasonable
  chastity.
They breed, asking for sons with unthinking hardihood;
the weaker die, the stronger arrogantly live,
walking from plain to mountain, where the early
  snow winds give

their strength to the nomad fire built of wild birch
    wood
by rock, in forest, in flowers, or sheltered by glacier
    stone,
left as a mark in the morning when the camp is
    broken and gone.

THE ANIMALS

All summer the fattening buffaloes move contentedly
    over
the glades of celandine and clover
and, high, on the highest alp's pyramid pinnacle,
are the goats. The goat boys' whistle
drops down to the rocks where the wild marmot sits
    up and begs
and screams aloud; the brood mares, white and dap-
    pled and red, lift their necks to listen while their
    foals stand straddle and try their newborn legs.
The flock-maned foals are darker, moles and creams,
    with a fluffy pampas tail and milk-wet nose;
they learn to crop the blossoming grass and share
    with kids and little buffaloes.
At night they go into the herdsmen's huts or stay out
    in fold, hobbled and huddled,
press flank into sleepy shoulder, sunk tail against shut
    head.
The summered night is warm, wind-absent, spread
in blue and cloud,

a common with the shepherd spirit, intransigent and
proud.

THE GOAT CHILDREN

The goat children are out on the grass
on the dales and the flowery slopes,
running barefoot over the grass
like little antelopes.
The girls have plaits or snoods
or caps with flaps or hoods
the shapes of bells.
The boys have tunics or ragged coats,
they run with or without their goats
but
they have goat manners,
and they have goat smells.

They bring wild currants and raspberries
to sell at a cutthroat price,
they bargain with bowls of raspberries
for annas and copper pice.
They live on rice and buffalo milk
and quarrel and boast and fight and sulk
as fiercely as cockerels;
they live on buffalo butter and curds,
their eyes are soft as their dark-eyed herds
but

they have goat manners
and they have goat smells.

THE GOAT BABY

Perhaps he had been born
at the height
of the pass,
at night
under the stars
or out upon the grass,
so that the open skies met his eyes' first open sight
as they laid him in his blanket among the primulas.

Perhaps it was at dawn
in the forest
when the birds
in nest
had not woken
and the multitudinous herds,
bleating low, lowing round, as he found his mother's
  breast,
from their folds below the fir trees had not broken.

A dark brown gypsy baby,
his first washing was in the snow streams,
his first sight the sky
and lost among the bleating kids, his first cry.

65

He will grow to herd the goats with other gypsy boys
exactly like him, dark brown boys,
with a saddle and blanket for dreams
and the ranges of all these wide mountains for toys.

MOVING DOWNWARDS

Summer has melted the ice, snowbridges dissolve and
    are gone,
the icebergs have grown small and float, thin, bright
    as jewels in the lakes; September comes, and on
the pass the snow winds gather; snow is in the air.
The valley grass begins to turn, swept of flowers, gold
    and bare.
There is no frost but the thick dew lies late; the streams
    are shallow and run quietly round the rocks.
The shepherd fires shine lower in the dark, the tribe is
    moving down before the blizzard blows and blocks
the passes, and the pastures are frost-bitten end to end.
    The sound of bleating comes on air that stings,
a dog's bark rings,
made sharp, made fine,
and the evening cold and early dusk are tempered with
    the hot torch scent of burning pine.

The flocks go past with the herdsmen, bearded, Bib-
    lical;

they make their camp on a Bible river of rushing
    crystal.
The unloaded hobbled ponies hop to graze,
goats nibble the grass; the Elders smoke their pipes
    and laze.
It is good to sit
as the fires are lit
and the women go to fetch water and wood;
the fires burn in a circle of stones as the food is cooked,
lentils and unleavened bread, roasted kid and rice.
The babies whimper, children play, young men lean
    lordly on their staves to gossip, or they wrestle to-
    gether or dice.
The tents are there,
the smell of cooking and wood smoke and animal dung
    fills the air.
Behind the passes, in the high camps left, flakes fall
and settle; the circle of the peaks is hidden; no small
live rustle will break the silence till the nomad spring.
On, on their downward journey the caravans endlessly
    swing
by day, by night,
with ponies, herds, dogs, babies, tents, blankets, and
    cooking pots, far down and out of sight.

The Red Doe

They were riding down from the upper pastures to get Ibrahim married.

Ibrahim felt pleased and important. There was only one person whom Ibrahim knew or felt anything about, and that was Ibrahim, the son of Ali the old herdsman; naturally the morning was pleasant and important to him.

It was so early, as they rode, that the grass in the valley far below showed in sheets of pale dew in the sun, and the ice streams shone, pale too, and bright with the early reflection of the sky; later in the day it, and they, would be a deep August blue and the grass would unroll, mile after mile, with the belts of coloured flowers that came in spring and summer; here spring was June, July, summer lasted a month, October brought the first snow, and the rest of the year was winter; these were the high mountains of the northwest Himalayas that led into Ladakh or Little Tibet.

The Red Doe

When the cavalcade of young men reined in to rest their ponies, whose legs shook from the steep way down, Ibrahim could feel and smell snow in the wind; it blew from the peaks that towered all round them on the skyline. Snow sometimes came in summer—"But not today," said Jassoof, Ibrahim's friend, laughing. "You don't want frostbite today, eh, Ibrahim?" The mountains ringed the valley, their sides sheer of rock and slate and pumice, snow on their peaks, their gorges filled with rubble and ice, and the great, wide, brown-white glaciers crawling to the river. Ibrahim could see eagles flying in endless circles below the crags, and he thought, watching them, It is windy there. He could hear the waterfalls that looked, from far away, like the crystals he found in the streams and sold in towns and villages on the way back to the plains.

Ibrahim's people were *Bakriwars*, goatherd nomads who drove their flocks up every year to summer on this rich alpine grazing. They moved in clans, each with its Elders. Ibrahim's clan had its encampment on an alp thousands of feet above the valley, in the last spruces of the forest where a small meadow spread its gentian and primulas and anemones and geums in the grass. Ibrahim did not notice flowers; they were part of the grass to him, grazing for his father's goats —as he did not see the colours of the glaciers, the wicked blue of the crevasses, the mountains or the

69

snow-slopes of the passes; he only knew how many marches away each was, which led to fresh grazing grounds, which snowbridges would hold. If he saw the eagles it was only to judge the wind; deer were for hunting with spears, bears were to be avoided, and the little wild marmots, who sat up on their tails to scream at humans, were for him and his friends to throw stones at. Ibrahim knew goats and ponies; he did not count them as animals but as his life; he lived with them as he lived with his father, mother, uncles, cousins, friends, especially Jassoof, but they were themselves, he was Ibrahim; he was not responsible for them, he had nothing to bother him, but now the time had come for him to have a wife.

"We want a good strong one," his father had said. He had said that too of the Yarkandi pony they had bought last year. "Not too young a girl, not less than fifteen, and strong."

Ibrahim had nodded and felt a sudden curious tingling that seemed to come in his palms and his thighs and the backs of his knees, and his throat was suddenly parched. "I want her to be beautiful," he said.

"Beautiful!" cried his father shrilly. "A beautiful woman is nothing but a nuisance. No, she must be strong, not too young, and of good stock."

"And beautiful," said Ibrahim obstinately, and his father leaned forward and slapped him on both cheeks.

Ibrahim was a young cock among the youths of the clan, but his father still slapped him when he thought it would do him good.

After that Ibrahim looked at every woman he saw, wondering if she were beautiful. They all looked beautiful in the distance but that was the way they walked, straight from heels to head, keeping themselves to themselves. Now Ibrahim's eyes came prying among them and he saw things he had not seen before: how their bare feet and ankles looked small under the folds of their black and red pleated trousers; how their black tunics swung out in skirts below their breasts, the full hems sewn and weighted with a load of white pearl buttons; how their veils hung loose but showed, under each, a flash of blue from the bracelet-size cap they wore on their heads; and how their silver jewellery sounded as they passed and repassed in and out of the huts and the tents, round the fires and through the flocks. Their anklets chinked, and their necklaces and earrings; Ibrahim began to hear that chinking in his dreams.

When the clan marched, the men drove the flocks, rode the ponies, and carried nothing unless it were a favourite child or a newborn kid. The women carried the gear of the camp on their heads, netted bundles of the heavy iron cooking pots and platters; they carried their babies in slings, or a child on a hip; they dragged the dogs on strings and drove the slowly moving, sick, hurt animals. They were also often in child-birth; the caravan was always having to stop and wait for an hour or two, or even longer, while a woman gave birth. Then the Elders were pleased; they liked to see the caps and hoods of the children running about in the clan, but the young men were impatient, though they often had to do the same thing with the herds. Ibrahim looked and wondered; some of the women seemed to him beautiful, none of them beautiful enough.

Now the day had come and he and his cavalcade rode down through the forests which grew more and more balmy as they came lower in the valley. Here there was a noise of wild bees and of larks above the meadows, where the larch and spruce trees opened on small alps of grass heavy with clover. The air smelled of resin and of honey. Ibrahim sniffed it and, sniffing, he found, suddenly, that he could smell himself.

He had been given a new turban of bright blue muslin, and he wore the wedding blanket, dark blue with fringes and a scarlet border, but his homespun coat was his own because he had no other coat, and he smelled of wool and wood-smoke and sweat and goat. To smell himself made him feel more than ever full of Ibrahim and more and more he felt that tingling excitement.

The chief moment of his life, up to now, had been when his father had bought him a saddle, but it was not a new saddle, and it was used by his uncles and cousins as well as by his father and himself. It was the same when he was given his first full-size blanket, the homespun, hand-woven blanket-shawl that all the men carried like a plaid on their shoulders; the blanket was not Ibrahim's, it was family property.

Now the tall young Jassoof led a small pony with an empty pad. Ibrahim, and no one else, would lead it back and his wife, probably for the first and last time in her life, would ride beside him, back up the mountain to her new home and she would be his own; no one would have the right to own her or use her except Ibrahim.

They were riding faster now that the path grew more gradual as it came near the valley. They rode like Cossacks on their small thick-set ponies, which were prized if they were short below the knee, well shouldered, with thick necks and thick manes. The mares had their foals trotting loose after them. Manes and blanket ends flew in the wind as they crossed the wooden bridge above the noise of the river, where it burst in thunder out of the mountain; the hoofs of the ponies made an equal noise on the wood. Spray blew in their faces and excited them and Jassoof let out a cry, a whoop, that made the others whoop like demons or wildcats to answer him, and the ponies plunged and broke into a gallop that swept them into the valley, with the ground drumming under the galloping hoofs. Then, at the far head of the valley, where a glacier spread and melted in streams across the grass, they saw a single dark speck, a hut.

Thick, loud whoops came from every young man round Ibrahim, jokes cracked across him, and they all began to whip their ponies. Ibrahim's grey kicked out, though he had not touched it, and broke away from the rest into a glade where mares and foals, running wild, were grazing on clover and forget-me-nots. Ibrahim knew he had seen the glade before; something else he had seen but he could not remember what; then it came into his mind that it had been when he was riding and that it had been exciting too, but another excitement. They had been hunting. Hunting? And then he remembered. It was a doe, a red doe, which had run, startled, out of the spruce trees, in front of them into this glade.

He remembered the shout that had gone up from the men and it seemed to him the same shout that was in his ears now; the whips had been lifted then too and the ponies were lashed as they spread galloping in a circle to head off the doe, while the older men, who had the spears, held them ready. Ibrahim had come up with the doe as she turned, driven back; he had come so close that he could see her red sides heaving for breath, her ears pressed down, and her muzzle strained as she ran. Ibrahim had swung his pony onto her and she turned again but sideways, and the old man, his father, had thrown his spear, and she fell, pinned through the neck to the ground. It was Ibrahim who jumped from his saddle to cut her throat before she died.*

There was something else he could remember that he did not want to remember, and he reined in his pony and rode slowly, step by step, through the glade. He did not want to remember, but he did remember. He remembered himself bending down with the knife in his hand and he remembered what he did not want to remember, that the doe, with blood gushing from her neck, had looked at him and then he was alone with her. No father, no Jassoof, no others were with him then; it was only Ibrahim and the doe, and he, her eyes knew, had done this to her. Suddenly, it was he who had been stricken, not the doe, because he was not Ibrahim, himself, any more, he was Ibrahim and the doe.

"Allah! Kill it!" shouted his father. "Owl! It will be dead before you cut!" And, dazed, Ibrahim had taken his knife and killed her.

When she was dead she was dabbled with blood to her scut; her small pale tongue hung out with blood welling still from her mouth; her eyes slowly glazed, hiding their meaning, but all day he could not forget. Perhaps he had never forgotten, but now, as his pony

---

* *Mohammedans can eat meat only if the throat of the animal is cut while it is alive.*

began to trot out of the glade, went into a canter, then to a gallop as it joined the others, he chuckled; he had remembered he had refused to eat the venison that night and that seemed to him, now, exceedingly funny.

They came to the hut. It stood by itself at the foot of the glacier on a fertile grazing plain fed by a hundred ice-springs. There were silver birch trees and flowers; buffaloes and goats were grazing. Other huts and tents stood on the edge of the forest and everywhere the smoke from cooking fires was going up. Children stopped to watch these stranger men on their little horses as they splashed through the stream and rode in a circle round the hut, faster and faster with cat-calls and whoops, as the Elders and the men of the clan came out to meet them.

The feast began. Inside the hut the fires were smoking and the men sat in a circle, dipping their hands into the iron bowls and platters of pilaff and roast kid and *chapattis* and apricots stuffed with mutton, and curd and honey rice. Ibrahim, feeling young and oddly light and thin, was put in the place of honour between the Elders and he was grateful that he should be silent as became a young man. He was shy but he was also very hungry. The food was good and he ate until he felt his stomach expanding and his legs growing warm and well-being coming up his back into his neck and face, so that he began to smile, feeling jovial again and suitably old.

All the young men knew where the women were. There was a cloth stretched tightly across the hut, nailed from wall to wall, that kept bulging and swelling as bodies pressed against it and, from behind it, came a continual sound, whispering and giggling and laughing, and that soft chinking of jewellery. Ibrahim looked and felt more than ever warm and jovial. The tea bowls came round and the *hookah*, the water-pipe, with its gentle liquid bubbling sound passed from hand to hand. Ibrahim thought that, through the cloth, he had caught a gleam of scarlet; wedding clothes were scarlet trousers and tunic, with a dark veil and new cap and new jewellery that chinked, chinked, as Ibrahim had heard it in his dreams. She was young—he knew that because she had been born in the same year as himself, the year of the great snow—and she was sworn to be strong, but Ibrahim was thinking now of a woman's skin, and he knew that he had seen it without noticing, and he marvelled as he remembered how it was fine, soft, much softer and finer than his own; he thought of a woman's hair and knew he had seen it loosed, another woman hunting in it for vermin and combing it, long and blue-black in the sun; he thought of a woman's body, of his body and hers, hers soft where he was hard, hard where he was soft so that they matched, and he began to tingle and had to dig his nails into the backs of his knees as he sat.

The *hookah* went round and the bowls of tea; Ibrahim thought they would sit there forever and that it would never end. He took his turn at the pipe politely, he drank bowl after bowl of tea, he listened politely to the jokes, barbarous jokes that made the cloth shake; he smiled until he thought his cheeks would crack, and still it went on and on.

At last Jassoof stood up and now the time for politeness was over and the raw thing would be done. Now the Elders would lead out the girl and put her on the pony with the empty pad and Ibrahim would take its hair rope in his hand and ride away with her.

There were no more jokes, no giggles; silence had fallen on the hut. The men separated into two dignified groups; the chief Elder, with his aged face and sorrel-dyed beard in the centre of his, Ibrahim in the centre of the other. Presents passed and the bride's dowry, a bundle of clothes, two good iron pots, and a few coins, was given to Jassoof; Jassoof's young brother stayed behind to drive up five chosen goats. Now the men went outside and the Elder went behind the cloth. Presently he came back and with him, supported on two sides by women, came Ibrahim's bride. All Ibrahim could see was a bundled shape in a red blanket, and the top of a bowed head. The blanket was wound to her nose, she kept her head obstinately down so that the edge of the blanket met her veil.

Ibrahim longed for her to look up until, looking round, he saw the same longing on the faces of all the men standing round. Some had wives at home, some were not yet married, but as they looked at the red bundle they had the same look, hot and thick and longing, and Ibrahim felt furiously angry and resentful; had she looked up then, he would have beaten her when they reached home.

She did not look up. With soft, slow, small steps, quite unlike her ordinary woman's stride, she went to the pony with the Elder, who lifted her onto the pad and put the rope into Ibrahim's hand. The women began to call out and laugh, a few to weep; the Elder stepped back and stood, tall and courteous, while the girl's father looked with expressionless eyes away to the mountains and Ibrahim's friends began to bit up their ponies and tighten their girths.

Jassoof had Ibrahim's grey pony. Ibrahim stood with the rope in his hand while the girl sat on the pad, motionless, her head down. As he stood there, he began to run his hand up and down the pony's neck, a cross, impatient hand; he ran it up to the pad, down the neck to the head, up to the pad, and then he noticed that every time his hand moved near the pad, the girl shrank back. It amused him and he moved his hand more, brought it nearer her each time, nearer and nearer, so that first it touched her blanket, then the soft folds of her trousers and then, unexpectedly, warm and firm, her thigh. The round warmth and firmness of it astonished Ibrahim so much that at first he left his hand there through sheer surprise; an equally astonishing sweetness filled him, added to the warmth and thickness and longing, and then he felt her tremble. He felt her tremble, and at that, triumphant strength filled him and he pressed his hand hard against her until something warm and wet fell on the back of his hand.

It was a tear.

Ibrahim stood still. The drop lay on the back of his hand; as he looked at it, it seemed that the Elder and the father and Jassoof and the young men and the women disappeared. Ibrahim was alone with this girl, sitting helpless on the pony, and he had made her cry. The trembling fear passed from her into him. He did not want to be married, he did not want to take her away, into his home and his hut and his bed and the days of his life, he did not want to have anything to do with such a business. He dropped the hair rope and turned away as the pony veered round.

The Elder caught the pony and courteously returned the rope to Ibrahim, showing no surprise. Jassoof caught his shoulder. "Owl! Can't you hold your own wife?"

"I don't want a wife," said Ibrahim.

"You will tonight," said Jassoof.

Ibrahim mounted his pony and Jassoof pulled up the small pony beside him so that its nose touched Ibrahim's leg. A throng pressed round them and the calls and shouts sounded across the valley. Someone laid a whip lash across the ponies' tails and they started forward, jerking through the streams so that the riders were splashed knee high. Ibrahim saw the girl draw up her heels and her hands came out of the blanket and clutched the pad. They began to gallop over the grass, all filled, all comfortable and jovial, feeling themselves more men since the morning, pleasantly fillipped and excited. The married ones began to think of their wives, the young ones eyed Ibrahim's and wondered when their turn would come; gradually the feeling spread to Ibrahim. The girl sat hidden and inert but, under the blanket, she was there, as warm and round and firm as the promise of her thigh, and presently he, Ibrahim, would undo that blanket.

He knew that, but he knew that he could not be only Ibrahim again: and, as they rode back into the red doe's glade, he knew that what had started in him with the doe was in him with the tear and would be in him now forever.

All the same he began to laugh as he led the way home.

The Little Black Ram

"Your mother was a prostitute, the daughter of a prostitute!" The children called that after him and the Elders and the women cried, "Shaitan! Seed of evil!" Jassoof did not care; his father was dead, he had no mother, and his tongue was so quick that he could give them worse abuse than they gave him.

The clan prized courage, spirit, and hardihood as they prized endurance and strength, but they were gentle and had the shepherd spirit; Jassoof, born one of them, was as different as if he were differently coloured, a firebrand with no sense of reason; he was a young thief, a bully, noisy, quarrelsome, and turbulent, against everyone with everyone against him. "What shall we do with him?" sighed the Elders. Only Ezekiel, the oldest of them all, thought something could be done. "He will learn," said Ezekiel.

"But when, when?" asked the exasperated Elders.

"Presently," said Ezekiel. That did not solve the

question of the fights among the boys when Jassoof
was sent to help with the grazing, the upsets among
the ponies when he was sent to drive with the men,
the milk stolen from the buffaloes, the calves panic-
stricken from his chasing when he was sent to keep
the herd, the food stolen and the girls teased when he
was left at home. Jassoof had no kinship with anything
or anyone unless it were the clan's self-contained, self-
reliant goats with their wicked yellow eyes and strong
horns. "*Bhai*"—"Brother"—one of the boys might
by accident call him in the warmth of play or work
and he always retorted, "I am not your brother. I have
no brothers."

Only, once, when he was lying on a rock, drumming
his heels in the sun, putting back his head to feel the
air on his face, shaking his black curls back from his
short, broad forehead to look up at the vault of the
sky and dare the sun with his eyes, did he hear a sound
that made him become suddenly still; it was a pipe
that Mahmud had brought up from the plains and
kept in his waist knot and played to himself, a thin
bamboo pipe. As Mahmud played it, Jassoof could not
bear it; it gave him a feeling of piercing sadness and
emptiness so that he did not know what to do with
himself; it made him too much alone, a speck on the
mountains, a nothing, a grain among a million million
grains; he wanted to go and look into the face of another boy, to go near him if it were only to kick him,

or to clasp one of the great goats round the neck even if it turned its horns on him. Mahmud played on and the feeling swelled in Jassoof until he felt he would crack in pieces with it and he jumped down off the rock on Mahmud and began to beat him.

"My pipe! My pipe!" Mahmud screamed, but the pipe was crushed against the rock as they rolled over. Mahmud's turban came off, Jassoof lay on Mahmud and pommelled him, an elbow on his chest, his hand holding Mahmud's hair while the other fist drove unfairly into his soft sides and belly. That made Jassoof feel himself again and his eyes looked as wicked as the goats'; when the other boys dragged him off, Mahmud was half stunned and bleeding. "You rascal! You good-for-nothing! You young cock!" said Abdul Kharim, the chief Elder, when Jassoof was sent for. Abdul Kharim slapped him on both cheeks and sent him a five days' march with old Ezekiel, who, besides being the oldest, was the crossest man of the clan, to buy sheep and drive them back.

"Sheep?" said Jassoof in disgust.

"Sheep!" said Ezekiel. Jassoof thought that sheep did not please Ezekiel either.

The nomads seldom keep sheep; they breed small horses and buffaloes and goats, suited to movement and enduring the steep and difficult climbs of summer pasturing; sheep are too slow, too soft for this, but occasionally, just before the clans move down, the

Elders will buy a few sheep to fatten and sell in the plains for the Indian autumn festivals. These were small, fat-tailed sheep, prime for mutton and for wool; Ezekiel and Jassoof drove them back and, before the first day was over, Jassoof hated their soft, woolly, helpless bundled bodies and their bleating voices. "Take care, young owl!" said Ezekiel, giving him a box on the ear. "Would you have that ewe in the river?" Though his ear was tingling, Jassoof shrugged and scowled and then laughed scornfully; he would have put the whole flock in the river. Ezekiel gave him another blow to teach him manners.

Late that night the same bleating ewe was delivered of twin lambs; one of the lambs was black. "Here, Shaitan, here's a brother for you at last," said Ezekiel, lifting it.

The black lamb, still with its cord hanging, red and wet, its legs dangling, lay in Ezekiel's hand. It had barely drawn breath, but struggled fiercely to get away and tried to kick with its tiny hoofs that were cloven and black. Its forehead, where the black curled hair was still sticky and damp from the birth was, indeed, very like Jassoof's but on its head it had the mark of embryo horns; it was a ram. "Take it and keep it warm," said Ezekiel, "while I see to the mother. Warm the other one too."

Jassoof picked up the white-grey lamb without interest but, when he put the black lamb under his coat and felt it move against him and butt him with its head, he was filled with a feeling that was the opposite of what he had experienced from Mahmud's pipe; he felt stirred, not to emptiness but, as he warmed the lamb, as if he were filled. When he felt its warmth he felt the warmth of himself, Jassoof. He looked down at the small curled black head nuzzling in the rags of his coat and he was puzzled to find that this feeling was good.

After that he and the ram were inseparable. It was not, Jassoof said, that he liked the ram but that it liked him; he pushed it away and even threw twigs and pebbles at it but it followed him where he went. It would not stay with the sheep but went after him among the goats and was not in the least afraid of them. It could balance on its small hoofs as well as any of them; its legs grew as strong as springs, and its body grew hard. "Allah! It will be tough eating," said Ezekiel.

The boys teased Jassoof, which made him angry. When the clan moved back to the plains, they taunted him with the butcher. "Butcher. Butcher will take your ram." Jassoof half wanted the ram to go; the boys threw stones at it and that made another unaccustomed feeling rise up in him, though the throwing back of stones was customary enough. The thought of the ram stoned, or slaughtered by the butcher, made his stomach feel queer. He wished Abdul Kharim would order something quickly but in the end the Elder did not send the rams to be killed and, when the spring came and the flocks were driven back to the Himalayas, the ram was with them, trotting at Jassoof's heels. When it felt the mountain grass under its hoofs and smelled the snow wind scented with honey from the flowers, it went wild with joy. It jumped with all four feet off the ground as it went cavorting and shying over the glades, shaking its neck and small fat tail with ecstasy. Jassoof suddenly laughed aloud, and in the same glee lay down and rolled in the flowers himself.

It grew large and strong; the hard small curves of its horns showed; and now, for the first time, Jassoof felt how troublesome the tiresomeness of another could be. On the strong mountain air and grass, the ram grew wicked; it would run at the women carrying their water-pots from the streams, and raced among the children, sending them flying; the women clamoured for it to be killed or sent away. Abdul Kharim looked and heard and frowned, the boys threw more stones at it; everyone was against it and still it went bounding, kicking, and butting round in the camp among the flocks, a small black tornado. "Take that black devil away from the folds." "Aie! It has broken into the hut and eaten the fresh curd." Then it ran at Rahman's Bibi when she was fully pregnant and she fell and had a premature birth; the baby lived but the anger broke out more fiercely. "Slit its throat. It should be killed. Ill-begotten. Seed of evil. Shaitan!" The feeling rose in Jassoof again, mingled anger and queerness; the queerness was that he felt that he was no longer Jassoof alone, but Jassoof and the ram, and again it was like the feeling from Mahmud's piping. He felt for it what he had not felt for himself, and he caught the ram by its neck and dragged it away from the camp to the goats. That night he did not go into the huts but slept out of doors with the goats and the ram.

Two days after that it ran at Daveed, a tall, big, sullen boy, almost a man, when he was riding an unbroken colt, which swerved in fright, throwing Daveed; even the women laughed while Daveed scowled, picked up a stone, and hurled it in temper at the ram. The stone, too large to throw at an animal, broke the ram's leg.

When any animal in the herd broke a leg, they sent for Ezekiel. If it was a clean break he, with his old clever hands, would delicately set it, splint it, and hold the splint in position with a crisscross network of light twigs tightly bound up the flank so that the whole limb was held stiffly when the animal moved; it was skilled work and took a long time. Now Ezekiel came and looked at the black ram. Jassoof felt himself tremble; no one liked the ram, they all wished it dead. Would Ezekiel cut its throat? "It's a clean break," said Jassoof and his tongue came out and licked his dry lips. Why could he not say a simple thing like that without having his tongue become dry and his heart beat?

Ezekiel grunted.

"It would not be—difficult?" asked Jassoof. The ram lay with its sides heaving in pain, moisture running from its nose. There was silence, till Ezekiel grunted again and, squatting down on his ankles, took twine out of the deep pocket of his homespun coat and began to work. He sent a boy for twigs and told Jassoof to hold the ram. "You are my father and mother," said Jassoof humbly.

The ram kicked hard with the other leg as Ezekiel pulled its broken leg straight. "Inshallah!" cried Ezekiel and swore at Jassoof for not holding it better. The boy pleaded under his breath with the ram to lie still, for he was afraid Ezekiel might grow cross and leave it but now he saw what patience the old man had; it is animal nature to kick and struggle against forcible pain and the ram struggled wildly, but Ezekiel went steadily on till the leg was straight in the splints and the network, woven with twigs and tied with twine, was so firm that even the most energetic ram could not kick it off. A reverence for Ezekiel began in Jassoof, who had never felt reverence for anything or anybody before; Ezekiel was taciturn and cross but had this power of healing which he would use for a bad boy and a plaguey young ram. When at last the ram was released it scrabbled with its feet on the ground and

89

quivered, blew through its nostrils, and stood upright. "In three weeks it will mend," said Ezekiel.

"God is great!" said Jassoof politely; his eyes glowed; at that moment he thought Ezekiel greater than God.

It was four days later that Abdul Kharim ordered that the clan should move, crossing the high passes that led down to the valley of the Liddar on the other side of the great range. "It is too late in the season," grumbled Ezekiel. "It is mad! The last pass is one of the worst in the mountains. If we get snow, there will be death. His father would not have done it."

They left the huts standing under the trees and began their march through the gorges and up the mountains to the passes. Day after day they journeyed on, passing rivers of water and rivers of ice, great glaciers perpetually frozen; climbing crags and precipices, wandering across high unknown glades, making a new camp each night, stopping sometimes for an hour or two for the birth of a child or of a late calf.

Jassoof, as he had the lame ram, was given the task of driving all the sick animals; usually only a woman or the mildest of the boys had patience to do this but now the fierce Jassoof left camp first in the morning and came in late, long after the others, sometimes long after dark. He had an old she-goat, once the leader of her flock, huge, old, tufted, ugly, and maddeningly obstinate; with her was a spotted half-grown goat as disobedient as she, and a small fat kid he had to carry. They all had broken legs, splinted like the ram's, and they walked, limping and hopping, stopping and whimpering, trying to lie down or break away. Only the black ram limped faithfully behind Jassoof and that made Jassoof go on and not rebel, though it seemed to him that each day was a moon of days; he lashed the old she-goat unmercifully but brought them all safely into camp each night. "That is a changed boy," said Abdul Kharim.

"I told you he would learn," said Ezekiel, smoothing his beard. Then he added, "But he will have to learn to do without the ram."

"But it is with the ram that he is good."

"He will learn to do without the ram," said Ezekiel. "One day he will have to learn."

They camped one evening not far from the foot of the last pass; its crags loomed over them and the night was cold, without stars. "Snow," said Ezekiel, sniffing the air. "I told them! Snow!"

Next day they were early on the march and Jassoof was soon left behind. That morning the old she-goat seemed possessed of the devil and the young goat followed her; it was not till long after midday that Jassoof drove them, dragging the kid in his arms, up among the rocks at the foot of the long cleft that led up to the pass.

He stood and looked at it, putting his head far back.

It towered for hundreds of feet over his head, sheer rock in which the wind, ice, and water had hollowed a curious funnel up which it was possible to climb on a spiral stair of great toothed rocks; it was steep and wildly rough. Eleven young men, with shouts and cries, were shouldering a buffalo up it; the buffalo panicked and lowed, but up it went, while the rocks gave the echoes back. The whole air round was filled with lowing and bleating and cries; there was pandemonium at the foot of the cleft; women were weeping; men sweated and swore, dragging and beating the animals. The boys were carrying up the kids on their necks; the goats went neatly their own way, but the buffaloes had to be pushed and lifted and the ponies swung by necks and tails from rock to rock. Slowly the crowd thinned and, from far up and out of sight, bleating and whistles dropped through the air and faded out of hearing.

As the afternoon went on, the light changed and flakes of snow began to fall; the flakes grew heavier and the work became feverish. Women, young men, and boys went up and down, up and down. Jassoof left his sick ones grazing and worked, carrying kids, pots, and bundles until his legs and back ached. One by one the other boys left and went on with the flocks, but Jassoof had always to return to his hurt animals. He knew they must be the last.

When most had gone he took up the kid and gave

it to another boy to carry while he came back for the half-grown spotted goat; but the step from rock to rock was too high for him to manage with its weight and if he dumped it on each rock ahead of him, it came down too hard on its injured leg. The men swore at him to keep out of the way and, crestfallen, he brought the goat back and waited. At last only he, two goats, the ram, and a pair of small white ponies were left. The snow was now falling so fast that Jassoof wondered what it would be like up on the head of the pass. "If it is a blizzard— Aie!" He rubbed his hands inside his knees and chafed his bare ankles, trying to keep warm, waiting for someone to come back. The animals quietly cropped the grass with the snow falling on their coats.

At last he heard men coming. There were four of them with the young Daveed. Jassoof sprang to his feet to help them. "It's big snow," they called to him and they started with the ponies, two men to each. "Hurry! Everyone has gone," they called. "We shan't get over if we are not quick. Quick. Hurry." Daveed swung the young spotted goat up on his shoulders. "Hurry. Come along, fool! What are you standing there for? Hurry. Be quick."

"But—these," cried Jassoof for the old she-goat and the ram.

"We won't wait for those. They are no good. She is old and he is Shaitan."

"But—" cried Jassoof running towards them, "they can't come alone." The ram, as it always did, came after him to see, butting him aside with its head.

"Leave them," called the men. "All that can't run are to be left. Hurry! Hurry!"

Jassoof's cry followed them. "I have brought them so far . . ."

"Turn them loose. Hurry."

"Come down again. Come back for us," called Jassoof.

One of the men turned round. "Little fool. You must save your own skin. Come on."

"Brother . . ."

Daveed's voice called back, mocking, "I have no brother."

Jassoof cried, "For the love of God . . ."

Nobody answered him.

Soon, far above, the voices and shouts died away. The quiet was eerie where the noise had been. The snow fell and the light dimmed to twilight. The old she-goat went back to her greedy cropping but the ram stayed by Jassoof; it was cold and wanted his warmth, its breath steamed over his hand. "Inshallah!" muttered Jassoof, bending to pick up the ram.

Its weight for him was tremendous, far more than the weight of the young goat. He staggered with it to the first rock and across to the second, but his arms were torn almost from their sockets while his heart

felt as if it would burst his chest. On the third rock
he had to dump the ram and he felt the jar as its leg
met the rock and heard its sudden surprised hurt bleat.
"Nahin!" said Jassoof and set his teeth and struggled
up with it once more and managed to get it safely to
the next rock, but the sides of the funnel and the snow
were whirling dizzily round him and he had to sit
down and put his head on his knees. "And there are
fifty rocks to get up, fifty, seventy, a hundred." Jassoof could not count but he remembered the rocks
leading up. The snow was coming thicker, blown in
gusts and eddies whirling in his face and choking him,
and it was not twilight now but getting dark. He could
hear the old she-goat bleating; she knew that she was
left. He sank his head down on his knees again.

"Ja-a-soof!"

"*Ye. Ye*," called Jassoof, springing up. "*Ye*. Come
down! Come down! There is one more. Come down."

"Come up," called the voice. "Hurry. Little fool.
Come up. You will be lost," called the voice. "You
will break your neck."

"Come d-own," called Jassoof.

"Come up. Come up. Come up." He could hear the
voice going away. "C-ome u-p, Ja-a-soo-of . . ."

All that he could see of the ram was a bulky black-
ness by his side, but he could feel it warm and close.
He bent and with another effort picked it up again.
Holding it against him for a moment, he looked up,

then turned back; struggling, slipping, dashing his feet against the stones, bruising his elbows and knees, he got it back to the foot of the cleft; there, sobbing for breath, he lay down, curled, letting the snow beat down on him lying still with the ram in his arms, but the animal did not understand and indignantly broke away, struggled and got up, bleating.

It was senseless to lie there alone. He stood up, a great fear sweeping over him. Numbed with cold, he shook his legs and shoulders, while the snow blew in his eyes and mouth. He looked up at the cleft again. There, somewhere ahead, if he could catch up with them, were his people, warmth and food. The she-goat had come back and stood with the ram, looking at him and waiting. Slowly, Jassoof unwound his short turban from his head and slowly wound it on again, winding the cloth over his head and ears, round his neck and over his mouth. The she-goat and the ram still stood waiting. Jassoof gulped and turned towards the cleft.

The old goat remained where she was but the ram at once hopped and scrambled after him. He heard it bleating as it tried to get up on the first rock; its hoofs scrabbled as it fell back. It bleated. Jassoof went on up the cleft. The bleating followed him a little way; then he could hear it no more.

Alone, he went up the cleft as easily and quickly as any strong young goat; the snow gusts hit him without hurting him, but he had another pain; almost breaking him was that same piercing emptiness and sadness that had come from Mahmud's pipe. There was nothing to break now but himself; the ram was gone.

As he found the top of the pass, he came out on a level cliff of rock and began to run towards the track that led down through the gathering darkness. The feeling grew until he felt he must break, and then there was a strange relief as he felt something on his face, drops of something warm and wet that appeared to come out of himself, out of that aching pain; strange drops, for when they were on his cheeks they froze to ice though when they came out of his eyes they were fresh and warm. As he ran towards the path they came faster, till they prevented him from running. He stood still while his tears fell fast.

III

KASHMIR

The Wild Duck

The wild duck came down on the river at dawn.

The river was the Jhelum in the Vale of Kashmir; it ran past the villages below the mountains into Srinagar, that water city with its seven bridges, its labyrinth of canals, the welter of high wooden houses on the banks in the snow, and its temples which rose in pagoda shapes with steps leading down, iced, to the water. Above the town, houseboats and *doongas*, native living boats, were moored under the *chenar* trees and the river ran by them softly, so held by the ice that the water was slow.

Winter comes with an almost Russian fierceness to Kashmir and, like the old Russian peasantry, the people are too poor and too oppressed to face it. There is no vigour in the Kashmiri in the cold; he hibernates. For five months in the year the land is sealed; except for necessity no one works, no one washes, and most people hardly wake. In the villages the houses are shut, the cattle closed into the ground floor so that the steam of their midden rises up and warms the rooms above. Even the boatmen close their boats down with mats and huddle inside in their vast shawls. Everyone —man, woman, and child—looks pregnant in Kashmir in winter because under the robes, against the stomach, a *kangri* is carried, an earthenware pot filled with live coals and held in a basket with a shielded handle. This is the fire-pot, which the Kashmiri keep with them, carry out with them, take to sleep with them, and which makes it possible to them to live through the winter though it inhibits every movement that they make.

In Subhan's boat, under the mats, the men slept and sat, with their fire-pots and their shawls, talked a little, and drank tea. At dark they went to bed and it was late into the day before they woke. Why should they wake? There was nothing to wake them. Khaliq, the eldest son, heard his wife get up; she was an inconvenient woman and needed to go out, but he turned again with his face to the side of the boat and slept. His wife went out onto the bank in the dawn and in the dawn the wild duck came down.

The winter dawn broke late and when it had broken nobody saw it; the people still slept. Khaliq's wife scurried back to bed and the bank was silent. Even the domestic ducks, each tethered by one leg, slept with their heads turned and sunk in the feathers of their backs. There were hundreds of ducks along the river and it was fitting that the first light showed duck colours: cream mottled with grey and brown and the bottle-green colours of duck necks. The grey was in the hulls of the boats, the browns in the mats that hung along their sides, while the snow was trodden to cream-brown slush on the banks. There was more grey in the trunks of the *chenar* trees and darker brown in their winter nuts; grey steps led to the water and there was grey in the sky with a promise of snow; even now, in the dawn, one occasional flake came down silently upon the water. The green was in the water, thick, translucent; dark green like a drake's neck feathers, turning to black under the boats, turning lighter, more lucent as it lapped the steps; green, cold, dark with ice. The wild duck came down upon the green as silently as the snowflakes; she folded her wings along her back and rocked a little on the water as she settled.

She did not realize where she had come; anything she might have known was blotted from her by her hunger, for she was starving. She immediately turned herself tail upwards in the water and her bill dabbled frantically in the weeds. She found what she wanted; the weeds were heavy with particles of ice but they were not frozen, there was life and food amongst them, and the wild duck went down and came up, came up and went down, and the point of her tail was

103

continually turned up to the sky that was slowly filling with the day.

She came up, dipped, came up. She had no feeling but of hungry emptiness; she was simply a duck, wild, come out of the winter sky, attracted by the weeds, and she had found her food; the river here was warmer, free of ice, warmed and broken by its life of boats.

There were houseboats, *doonga* cook-boats where the boatmen lived attached to the houseboats, wood-boats, rice-boats, grass-boats, ferry-boats, little boats; later in the day some would be poled along, handled under the bridges, or paddled from side to side. All along the banks the litter of human beings lay silently in the coming light; dogs, bicycles, woodpiles, water-pots, tethered geese and fowls. Presently, from one boat and another, the first wood-smoke went up.

Close by there was a village of tall houses with over-hanging balconies and a tall, thin screen of poplar trees; now from the village came the sound of clogs stamping on the ice, of a tap opened and water splashing on the ground. The wild duck came up and stayed motionless on the water with her head turned on her neck to the sound.

The village was upstream and upwind; the alarming sound floated down but the current of the water still parted steadily around the duck, still steady, still undisturbed. The current reassured her; she paddled with her feet to keep her place; her feet were the colour of the orange peel that floated down in the debris of the river.

The sun had risen now and the watery winter light picked up fresh colours from the life on the river: the colour of the orange peel, the dress of a child who scooped up water in a *samowar*, the Kashmiri tea-urn, out of the river; the light caught the copper colour of the urn and the jewel blue in the wild duck's wing; the blue distinguished her from the ducks by the boats, the tame, tied-up domestic ducks, fattening themselves with sleep and scraps and tidbits out of the weeds.

The weeds were a feast to the wild duck. To the west, where she came from, the lakes were frozen, the reeds embedded in ice; reeds and wild iris blades and the bare muddied shores were stiff in a shroud of it. The hills at the foot of the mountains were brown and withered as if they were scorched with the cold, and the water in the rice fields was covered with a casing of ice in each field. The only life and movement was from the far nets of the fishermen where the current stayed unfrozen in the lake, and from the fires of the charcoal burners on the foothills, and the rumble and fall of an avalanche up on the distant mountain. The wild duck had come down for food; her hunger dulled her senses; she dipped and rose.

Then, in the boat, a mat was lifted and snow fell

into the water with a loud splash. The wild duck flew out of sight. No one had noticed her yet.

Khaliq came into the front of the boat and sat down in his shawl. He felt heavy and dull. He was young, lithe, strong, the finest, tallest man of a fine family, and a born boatman; his father was a boatman, his grandfather had been one, and his great-grandfather's father before him. They were *shikaris*, hunters, too; when they were not in their boats they were camped. They handled boats and guns; both were as natural to them as their own hands, but in the winter they sat with their fire-pots in their shawls.

Khaliq hated that. He hated the winter, the inaction, the heavy dullness in his bones. He was overladen with the winter and, as he sat that morning, suddenly, like a crack in its ice, a memory came back to him. Last summer he had been out ibex shooting, convoying an English colonel into Yarkand beyond Leh and the valley of the Indus; very far away, up and up in strange, far gorges, empty except for the flocks that nibbled dusty herbage at the foot of the hills, the eagle's occasional cry, and the queer—even to Khaliq queer—broken notes of the flutes the shepherds played.

They had come to a village grown out of the gorge, where the houses were made of its colourless earth; there a glacier came down, and the village had a grove of quince and mulberry trees. Khaliq remembered

1 0 6

how startling in that barrenness had been the colour
of their green. The colonel and he had left the tents
and the servants and gone up, up, up; two local hunters
hauled the colonel up the crags; Khaliq followed,
carrying the guns; Khaliq, loaded with the rifles, had
been the equal of the mountain men.

He remembered how, then, his body had been ful-
filled; it was quick, awake, intense; its power, its
speed, its sensation, its every fibre and nerve were
alive. Each movement of his body was as necessary
as an animal's; the parts that were beautiful and the
parts that were bad, the parts he enjoyed and parts
that troubled him were all drawn up into a supreme
wholeness; he was one, whole, for this supreme use.
Even his shoes were part of him, even the last hairs
of his moustache were necessary to the completeness
of this whole, beautiful, enduring Khaliq. They went
up and up into a giddy rarer air, and then one of the
local hunters pointed, and, following the line of his
brown finger, they saw an ibex an eagle's flight above
them, standing on a pocket of rock that showed,
through a cleft, a pocket of sky.

The hunter on the left of Khaliq said, "Aaah," in
his throat and the sound made a gulf in the abyss,
dropping down like a stone; Khaliq had moved an
angry hand but, as if the sound had truly gone down,
not up, the ibex did not stir. There had been a quality
of agony in that, a tension that hurt the breath more

than the height; the colonel was panting and Khaliq remembered how his own heart had hammered with thick, thumping, clumsy strokes that would have taken the breath of anyone less strong and whole than he.

The ibex was still there and, as they watched, the sun glinted on its horns and it lifted its head to show the tuft and sweep of its beard.

They had to track and pinpoint it. Up again, again up and up, when not a stone must roll and fall as had that sound; they were closer now, up and up, until through a split rock they saw a giddy slant of sky and crag—and the ibex. They had found a sight.

The ibex was below them now and they saw it with an eagle's eye; the planes of the peak were below them too, and the glacier that now had a blue reflection from the sky. They saw plane after plane of rock face, rock crag, land slips and, a sound more than a sight, the river far below. The ibex was feeding, unsuspicious, eating the tufts of herbage, and to see it eat as the goat-kids had nibbled in the valley gave Khaliq a sudden pain that was the tensest moment of living he had ever known. That simple thing of the ibex nibbling had parted a skin that had lain in his mind, a skin between the wild and the tame, and always after that tame Khaliq and wild Khaliq were integrant. He had said, speaking behind his lips to the colonel, "Now, Sahib. Keep low. A little to the left." There had been no mistake; while the sound of the shot still rang from rock to rock, the ibex had thrown up its head, fallen on its knees, and tumbled off the crag.

Why should Khaliq think of that now? All morning he kept thinking of it again. The memory kept coming up. His mind had hiccups and he could not quiet them.

The morning in the boat went on as did all such mornings; his father's friends and his own friends came in to sit and talk; the air grew thicker between the matted sides of the boat, the hookah passed, and there was comfortable talk about money. Only in Khaliq's mind the memory came up; the ibex and the climb and the crag against the sky. He saw the sun on the polished horns and the sudden blue of the glacier and it seemed to him impossible that he had ever seen them; he could believe in the feel of the horns as they lay in his hand after the ibex was dead, but had he seen them flashing in the sun? The colour of the glacier seemed strange, faint and far as hope. The village seemed like one of the villages in his father's tales; had he, Khaliq, been there only a few months ago, seen the green leaves of the mulberry trees, pitched his tent, and bought wild honey from the people? He put away his fire-pot; it seemed too hot, it bothered him, and the folds of his shawl were heavy on his shoulders; he let it fall on the floor beside him as he sat, but immediately he was cold and had to put it on; and while they were talking the wild duck came down again and settled on the water near the boat.

The river's own tame ducks were loosened now; they were swimming up and down in tidy convoys, leaving a pointed wake behind them. As soon as the wild duck came down they came to her and swam around her, and immediately their shapes looked clumsy and dull; they were no longer tidy and pleasing, they were platitudinous, overwhite or wrongly plumaged with the darkened colours of their wings and necks.

The wild duck rocked among them; except for the movement of the water she was utterly still and seemed to be floating in the water, not lying in it stoutly as they did. She was still; she paddled her feet but she did not move her eyes. As if she withdrew for choice, her feathers seemed to fit her closely; she looked small, light, graceful, and the colours of her markings, stronger than those of the mottled tame ducks, were definite and clear in the winter daylight; the deep blue bar in her wings flashed in their eyes. Resentment spread in a ripple round her but she still paddled her feet and rocked lightly, lightly as the ripples grew.

In the boat the air grew closer and more odorous; the hookah passed to Khaliq and he inhaled it with a melodious bubbling of its water, but it did not soothe him. The talk went on and he slumped with discontent, silent in his corner. "Khaliq does not say a word," said Mohammed, his friend.

His father, Subhan, looked at him. "By his colour

he is cold," said Subhan. "He looks that he is sick."
And he called through the partition, "Bring Khaliq
some good hot tea."

Khaliq said not a word and presently Mohammed
began to play on his two-stringed zither. It made a
noise like a tortured violin, and the noise in the
shrouded boat was near and very loud. Khaliq's wife
brought a bowl of salt tea from which a spiral of steam
and a smell of spice went up. She pressed it into
Khaliq's hand; it was very hot, the heat came through
the sides of the bowl against his palm and irritated
him; more heat, more soothing, more allaying, more
deadening down when he wanted not to be dead, when
he was overdead, when his mind strained to be alive;
and the maddening little tune of Mohammed's bow
went on around his ears. The noise and the heat and
the closeness clashed suddenly in Khaliq's head; he
gave a cry and threw his bowl of tea across the floor.

There was consternation, a silence that was more
wracking than the music. Subhan cleared his throat
and his face under his old folded turban was outraged.
It was incumbent on Khaliq to explain; there must be
something said, some explanation, something. "Disgusting," cried Khaliq. "The tea was disgustingly cold."

Relief and happiness. The tea was cold. What, to
give the boy cold tea when he was sick and chilled!
There was immediate shouting to the wives, scolding
them, a jangling of earrings and whispers in the next

compartment of the boat, and an immediate dipping of the *samowar* in the river to be refilled.

A child was sent to dip. He had to put his head outside and, as he bent, he saw the conglomeration of ducks across the water; he watched with the *samowar* in his hand, and a flake of snow fell directly down upon the wild duck's back. The child saw the flash of brighter blue, the small neat shape, and his cry went up, "*Arman Batukh*, wild duck, wild duck!"

This time Khaliq did not betray himself. The cry went through him as if it were a spear thrust, but he said nothing. He simply put his shawl down, stood up in one movement from his heels, and was gone, swiftly but with no look of haste. He was no quicker than Mohammed, who was out on the prow of the boat, loosing the small paddling boat, the *shikara*, though it was Khaliq who stepped to the prow. His father handed him a barbed spear and sent the light boat shooting out to the ducks in a thrust that was the real counterpart of the cry that had pierced Khaliq through.

Now they were out in the river, Khaliq standing balanced on the prow and Mohammed sitting paddling in the stern. The boat was narrow and light and Mohammed's heart-shaped paddle broke water with hardly a sound; he kept the handle away from the side while Khaliq stood, poising the spear like a harpoon.

They sped towards the ducks, Khaliq balancing from foot to foot, tightening his muscles, tautening, loosening, alive and ready. The speed of the boat, the intentness of his eyes made a blur of the banks, the water, the sky; the sky was in the water, the water in the sky, there was again that giddy sense of height, planes spun below him, reflected planes; sky spun above him, but there was only one small object, small as the bead of a gun, in front of his eyes.

The wild duck had her attention on the tame ducks; they were a new experience for her and acted as decoys, swimming round her, paddling the water with their orange feet as she did, but not stationary, swimming round and round. She watched them and her wariness, usually erect as the antennae of her tail, was lulled by lesser danger. She was bemused and unconscious of herself as she watched the ducks.

The spear hurtled into them. It came with a deadly aim, strong with speed, straight at the wild duck's breast. The breast half rose in the water to meet it, half too late; a domestic white duck had risen before it with a quack that was to ring in Khaliq's ears for days and nights, a quack like the flat of a hand in his face. His own hand was empty, the spear had gone, and the white duck flapped and cried; through the end of its outstretched wing the spear had passed, deflected, only deflected, not turned from its path, and one barb had struck the wild duck's breast, tearing the feathers. A morsel of flesh fell with them into the river where the spear furrowed a wave, was brought up, and lay harmlessly floating in the water.

The boat was carried on; by its impetus it shot away to the farther bank, towards the mud and snow.

The wild duck struggled in the water and blood oozed from her breast in a thick trickle that immediately changed to a stream in the water; it was dark on her breast, clear and scarlet in the stream. She struggled and dipped sideways to the weeds while the white duck made loud rending noises, as loud as the shouts from the boats and the bank.

The exhilaration of the wind had died down from Khaliq's ears; the world had settled into its accustomed places as the boat struck the bank with a thud, driving into the snow.

"You have it," cried Mohammed, looking back.

Mohammed was never accurate; he said what he hoped would become true, but at that moment the wild duck gave a cry and rose into the air; she rose with a clumsy motion, splashing, scattering drops of water, but her wings, even on the wounded side, could fly.

The white duck flapped but the wild duck lifted and flew; her cry floated down with the solitary flakes of snow, a single cry that was mournful, wounded, wild. The tame ducks paddled and eddied round the place where she had been and the stain of blood was washed out on the current; they dipped their bills looking for her, turning indifferent tails upon their wounded comrade.

Already from his boat the owner of the wounded duck was paddling out to parley with Khaliq, and already Subhan, as Khaliq's father, was coming in a borrowed boat to defend his son and dispute the price. Mats were lifted up and down the river, waiting for the quarrel, and Khaliq's wife was quickly brewing the second tea with extra spices to soothe the episode away.

Mohammed turned the boat to go back for the spear and Mohammed was silent. Khaliq knew it was for him to speak; but he was sealed; his face had settled into a sulky despair. Mohammed paddled, waiting.

"I thought I had it," said Khaliq with a mighty effort as he knelt to get his spear. That was all that he could say. He could not laugh.

Two Sonnets

KASHMIRI WINTER

Big Sister, Hungry Sister, and the Greedy Dwarf of
    Ice,
these are forty days of winter, then twenty and then
    ten.
Can we fight them with straw sandals? And the leaping
    price of rice,
of charcoal and of salt and tea? Nothing is cheap but
    men.

The sisters have taken lovers, the blizzard and glacier,
the goose-white flakes of snow in the sky perpetually
    falling.
Why does Rashid lie so still, so still? His fingers flutter
    and stir.
It is the sisters calling; calling; calling.

The gravestones are narrow and small, lost in the
    snow, but free.
We shall be landowners then, Rashid, with no taxes
    to pay.
He has shut his big owl's eyes, now his rags are worth
    more than he.

Strip him and put him into the earth whom the sisters
    have taken away.

    The iris leaves cover the graves; their spears
        will blossom between;
    green is the Prophet's colour, but the snow
        has hidden the green.

SPRING SONNET

Flash heaven! That is the kingfisher. This fall
of bronze, green-fingered, is the willow's spring.
No season's calendar pinned to the wall
but punctual every mood and colouring;

for yesterday the mountain slopes were shields
damasked with gentian, primulas, and clover,
the youth of almonds broke the mustard fields,
magnetic to their minute, they were over.

Then came the white wild tulips striped with rose
and others ringing scarlet in the grass.
Lilac and iris follow after, those
purple and white and white and purple pass.

    No feather falls; no sign to sharpen sight,
    to tell, this is the moment; this, the flight.

IV

JUNGLE

Mooltiki

Though I have spent years in India my knowledge of elephants is slight and purely domestic. I have never seen, nor do I want to see, a *keddah;* nor, as the rest of my family has often done, seen a herd wild in the jungle. I have not seen elephants dying, fighting, making love, or giving birth, all, I understand, highly mysterious processes. I know elephants only as servants.

When I was what in another country would have been the sitting-up perambulator stage I used to go for airings with my little Assamese nurse Butterfly on a big she-elephant inappropriately called Birdie. I can remember giving her a reward of some minute, picked blades of grass and leaves; it must have been like offering a human being two or three grains of salt but Birdie always took them politely.

Then there was Adela, an elephant attached to the household of a friend who was agent to one of the small states. No roads went to the palace and transport was by Adela, dignified comings and goings with suitcases. Rajah was my father's shooting elephant, and when my sisters and I grew up enough to acquire men friends, some of our courtings were done on Rajah. Just as couples go for long, aimless drives, borrowing the father's car, so we borrowed Rajah for long, leisurely rides, though the mahout was there, of course.

I remember a small elephant at the seaside in southern India. She was an elephant for hire, her chief engagements being to lend tone to marriages and feast days. She was advertised in the local paper as "docile she-elephant, used to walking in processions, ears pierced for ornaments." Then there were Secunda and Bata Scully, the two big elephants working for our friend Neil in the forestry department—and there was Mooltiki.

She does not belong in a list, for I think she was unique. My acquaintance with her was brief but I have never forgotten her. Neil, who, in a lifetime of elephants, was her owner, says he has never forgotten her either.

I met her when my sister, Nancy, her husband, Dick, and I went up to stay in the same Neil's winter camp in the Assamese jungle on the borders of Bhutan.

After a long, hot night in the train and what seemed an endless drive by lorry on the bumps and pits and ruts of a jungle road, we came out in a clearing on the river bank and saw the camp across the river. This was one of the wide rivers of the foothills, for the most part shallow with pale, pebbled shoals, then narrowing suddenly to fierce rapids. Tiger grass and forest lined both banks and, in the distance, were hills folded in a blue haze. "Bhutan," said Dick. The camp was on a sweep of land, looped by the river; we could see a tiny house on stilts that looked like matchsticks, four or five white tents, with encampments of lesser tents and a flagpole, small as a splinter. Smoke was going up from the fires and, coming to fetch us across the river, was a small grey shape. Even as it climbed out of the water and mounted the bank, declaring itself to be an elephant with a mahout on its back, it still looked small and it was grumbling to itself under its breath.

When Mooltiki had to do anything she did not like —and I have to admit that her days were filled with unpleasant tasks—she kept up this small, clearly opinionated, and private rumble. It was curious how potent it was. There was never any doubt of Mooltiki's feelings; as with other put-upon maids of all work, she would flounce and bounce, and to be flounced and bounced under when one is riding even a small elephant can be very uncomfortable indeed.

One of her tasks, as Adela's had been, was to fetch and carry baggage, stores, and passengers from the roadhead across the river. I sympathized with her;

three times that morning, for our luggage and stores alone, she had to cross that river bed, braving the rapids, treading gingerly across the shoals as if the pebbles hurt her feet, and hauling herself up the banks with a creaking of the ropes that held her pad. If she paused or slowed she would get a jerk behind the ear or a jab on the head from the mahout's *ankus,* a weapon that looked like a big iron hook with a spike.

I soon saw why it was needed; straightaway, when she knelt to let us get up, I made acquaintance with one of the less endearing traits of Mooltiki. A well-schooled elephant kneels when told and allows its hind legs to be used as a mounting block to the pad which is fastened by padded ropes round its neck and stomach and by a crupper under the tail. One can hold to these, spring, kneel on the rump, and swing up. Bata Scully, Neil's big she-elephant, would even lift her master up by her trunk, raising it carefully and putting her ears forward so that he could hold to them and walk up her face; not until everyone was comfortably settled and her mahout gave the word would she rise. Not so Mooltiki; out of her small eye, which looked deep and as many-sided as a camera lens, she would watch and, I am sure, mark her victim—every time it was a woman—and when that victim, holding to the ropes, had one knee on Mooltiki's behind, the second foot just off the ground, Mooltiki would heave herself up abruptly and walk away. To fall off an uncertain elephant is dangerous; quite apart from the bump, the animal may turn round and tread on one, and many a time I have been scooped up by Bangla, the head *shikari*, just in time or have had to hang with scraped hands until the mahout's shouts and stabbings produced an effect.

That morning we were tired and shaken, but she immediately tried this on me. Then, while we were still swearing, "Abominable elephant, dangerous little brute," she did something else, a thing I have not seen another elephant do: on the long way back across the river she amused herself. She held her trunk with its nozzle just below the water and, through that small, groping spout-mouth, divided into holes and lined with pinkish skin, she blew bubbles. The pebbles in the sun were grey, almost white, but under the water they took colours, brown with a blue gleam, here and there a cabbage green one or one that was coral red; the bubbles picked up the colours of the pebbles, of the wide pale sky, and shone, iridescent. It is only people who dream and wonder who blow bubbles, children and poets—Shelley blew them; there was something of child or poet in Mooltiki. I have known her, in the forest, to pick a flower, not a branch to beat flies off or a frond to wave as most elephants do, but a flower to hold.

It was autumn and the forest was dry after the hot weather; the only flowers were the white stars of wild

coffee and the red-flowering simul trees. Everywhere
were great blackened patches left by the forest fires
with which Neil was busy, and the smell of their smoke
and charred wood was strong on the air. Soon, on
these patches, sweet new grass would spring up, bring-
ing herds of wild elephant and deer to feed.

The house on stilts was a forest lodge, used now for
stores; the tents were drawn up in a semi-circle facing
the river, in their centre a campfire built with logs
and whole trunks of trees. The cook tent had its own
fire and an oven made of clay—we once roasted a pea-
hen whole in it—and the *shikaris*, the huntsmen, had
their own camp behind, two tents just big enough for
men to lie down in, a shelf woven of bamboo for holding brass platters and pots, clothes hung along a string,
and a tiger's tongue stuck on a pole to dry—tiger
tongues could be sold as a cure for goitre. The elephants
were farther off still, their leg chains around two trees,
the ground near them littered with leaves and elephant
pats.

At night the fires made the jungle seem infinitely
ringed off. We would sit in wicker chairs, warmth on
our feet but a gentle snow-wind, the evening wind off
the hills, touching our foreheads. There was a great
feeling of well-being. We were filled with whisky and
dinner and listened peaceably to Bangla and the plans
for tomorrow.

Bangla was a hillman, small, with tremendous hands

and feet and a short supple back. His skin was a ruddy polished brown and his face was Bhutanese, flat-nosed with deep eyelids and an intelligent forehead. He often smiled at our antics, but he was said to be a bad character. "He is a bloodthirsty cut-throat," said Neil.

"If I have to have my throat cut," I said, "or to be killed, I should rather be killed by Bangla than anyone else." He was amazingly quick and deft with a knife and to see him skinning a tiger's head was a marvel. He was, even Neil admitted, a good *shikari* and, though the slightly amused smile never left him, there was not a dreadful moment, on the ladder of a *machan*, on the slippery tail of an elephant, when Bangla's brown hand did not come out to help. There were three other *shikaris* in the camp and a cook, a table-boy, a washer-up, and a camp sweeper.

Neil had to work but Dick had come to shoot, with Bangla to help him. Bangla was as courteous as he was knowledgeable. If a plan seemed to him feasible he would say, "It could be like that"; if he had to criticize, "It could not be like that," and proceed to show how it could be. Often he drew maps in the dust. The voices went on, the smell of wood ash and flowers would drift in from the night, the whisky would pass and the peace deepen, peace such as I have known only in the jungle or on the moors. It was as deep as the jungle sky where the sparks from the fire mixed with the stars; but the fire would die down. Then Neil would clap his hands, an answering rattle of chains would sound from the elephant lines, and presently a sound would approach, a reluctant, slow pad-pad of feet, a flapping of ears, and a certain unmistakable annoyed rumbling. It was Mooltiki coming to make up the fire.

It was one of her duties to build and feed it; when we were out on her and riding home she would thoughtfully pick up a young fallen tree or a big branch and carry it in, bearing it across the path when the track was wide and neatly turning it end on where it was narrow. Usually, though, she did her wood-gathering after tea and would appear from the jungle at intervals, carrying a large log in her trunk, small branches or brushwood in her mouth which made her look as if she had a moustache, and would build a pyramid, laying logs one across the other, pushing them with her foot, and leaving a pile handy for the night. She would have to come two or three times in the night to put on wood.

"Is it really necessary?" I said.

"Well, you don't want a tiger or a leopard walking through us, do you?" asked Neil.

Now, as she kicked the logs together with a careful foot, shifted their ends with her trunk, Mooltiki said clearly and unmistakably what she thought of human beings who needed fires, by elephant standards quite unnecessary. Sometimes the wood ran out and she would have to go into the dark jungle to get more. The mahout would make her put her forehead against a small tree and push; with grunts and loud sighs Mooltiki would push until the tree cracked, when she would wrench it loose with her trunk and foot. Her mahout was strict; if she threw the log down when she brought it to the fire he would make her pick it up again and put it down more gently. Then she would walk back to her bed and leaf-supper, still saying what she thought of us.

There was one pleasant thing in the day for her and that was to be bathed. Every day the mahouts took the elephants to the river. Washing an elephant is easier than washing a car or an engine, for the hose is animated, and it was a sight to see the three elephants sending fountains of water running over their backs and heads and then lying on their sides, their feet outstretched, while the mahouts scrubbed them with a besom made of jungle twigs; Mooltiki's skin gave shudders of sensuous bliss. When she was scrubbed clean, her mahout would jump clear, shout to her to get up, and once again would begin those copious pourings; but, like a naughty child, Mooltiki would never come out, and often Bata Scully, who was older and wiser and almost horribly well trained, would be called on to give her a spank. Then Mooltiki would come out at once and walk, crushed, back to camp. She had a wholesome respect for Bata Scully, but Secunda never noticed her at all.

From the beginning I was much with Mooltiki because, in a way, we were both hangers-on, which is to say, nuisances. I did not shoot, nor was I taking animal photographs, working in forestry or botany, which is why I cannot write of the camp in any expert way, while, as a jungle elephant, Mooltiki had two grave defects: she was not tall and she was not staunch. A tiger spring would have reached anyone on her back though, as I pointed out, the tiger would never have got near enough to spring because, at the first sight or smell of anything fierce, or even if a shot were fired near her, she would bolt.

Mooltiki justified her existence by working hard. She was the camp tweeny and, besides carrying all the luggage and wood, she went to the post, ten miles inland, twice a week, and every day she fetched and picked part of the food for the elephants; as each elephant ate perhaps a thousand pounds of green stuff every day, this was heavy work and we would see her toiling backwards and forwards with trailing loads of cane and leaves. Except that I liked it, I had no excuse to be in the camp—until the coming of Horatius.

A tiger had been taking cattle from one of the forest villages and the villagers came to Neil to ask if he would shoot it. Neil passed them on to Dick, who asked me if I should like to sit up with him in a *machan* built in the forest near the village.

It was surely one of the most lost villages in the

world. To reach it we walked through the afternoon, on and on by the river, through grass higher than our heads, dry, dusty brown, and baking hot. At a blazed tree we struck into the jungle, walking in a nightmare forest under *sál* trees whose stems were patterned like giraffe necks; their enormous leaves in colours of beetroot and purple had fallen and rattled on the ground. In their branches were ants' nests made in shapes like great white cocoons and all round them creepers twined and hung; originally blown above the jungle, they had seeded in the tops of the trees and grew downwards in fantastic spirals and snakes.

We seemed to make a loud noise walking in the dry leaves but that was because the jungle was so quiet, quiet, dim, brooding, and, in the middle of this great tract, we came to the village, a desolate space cleared under the trees, four or five huts on stilts, a stockade and a patch of fields walled with mud. Even there the light was dim, filtered through the trees, and even the hens were quiet. In front of it was a row of whitewashed stones; one side of them was Assam, the other Bhutan. The villagers, small, brown, half-naked men, had built the *machan* and under it, for bait, they had tied Horatius.

He was young, not yet bullock, but not calf, about four feet high and exceptionally solid and heavy; he was black and had a hump and two swellings of horn. The villagers had tied a bell round his neck to attract

131

the tiger, and I tried not to look at him as I climbed past him up into the *machan*.

The rifles, a knapsack, pillows, and rugs were drawn up by rope, cut jungle was heaped round the ladder, and the *shikaris* went away, leaving us alone, and talking as they went to make the tiger, if he were near, think we had all gone. Even at half-past four in the afternoon we seemed very much alone, but the little bull was not perturbed. The sun was slanting its rays down the glade, the stems of the trees on the edge of the forest were lit, the light yellow and luminous between them, but it was growing darker in the jungle depths.

We arranged the *machan*. It was built high between three trees, a raft of cut branches tied with strips of bamboo and hidden with leaves; the smell of the dying leaves was pungent and forever afterwards that smell to me was exciting. The rugs and cushions were needed, for we might have to stay without moving till the morning. Sitting over a live kill is an art in stillness and even the sandwiches were wrapped in banana leaves that would not rustle; Dick had his and I had mine so that we should not need to speak to each other. Nothing white or conspicuous must show; the pillows had dark covers, we wore khaki and had thick coats and string gloves for, when the dew came, it would be cold. Dick fixed his torch on his rifle, I had a second rifle ready. All the time below us the bell tolled.

"It *is* cruel," I whispered. "I don't care what you say."

"Of course it's cruel, but it's one life against dozens if that tiger is left alive."

Dusk came down and there could be no more whispering. Squirrels ran down the tree and looked at us, making us start. It became dark very quickly.

A tiger usually comes early, soon after dusk, or else late, near dawn, seldom in the middle of the night. Slowly, over the forest, a listening stillness settled. The bell sounded, loudly in one moment, forlornly in another. Except for it the forest was tensely still. A leaf fell with a sound loud enough to be a tiger. Another fell after it. There was a heavy dot-dot-dot-dot, like hopping, far louder than a tiger; it was a jungle cock and his hens moving round the tree. All at once a noise came that paralysed me even though I knew what it was, a noise like a dog being torn in half, a barking deer. Again there was stillness and the bell.

Then the stillness changed. It was different. There was a root of terror in it—somewhere. The tiger was there. I could see nothing, hear nothing, though my eyes strained into the uncertain blackness; there was no sign except that the little bull was absolutely still. The expectancy went on. Something touched my cheek and I froze in horror; it was Dick's finger, pointing.

Where he pointed, with a shock of fear I saw it. If it had been lit with flares I could not have known more certainly what it was—tiger. I saw its shoulder before its head, the outline of its shoulder as it looked down the glade, a gigantic, exaggerated symmetry that reached up into the dark, that seemed to terrorize even the leaves into stillness. Then it turned its head, which brought it back into size so that it was quite near the ground, but I was even more deadly afraid of it like that.

"Why was I so afraid?" I asked Neil afterwards. "I was safe in the *machan*. Why was I afraid like that?"

"Because it was tiger," said Neil. "I am afraid every time, and how many tigers have I shot?" And he added, "A tiger carries fear. That is its power."

As its shape came forward I was still, though inwardly shaking. I lost it, saw it, lost it, then the bell was ringing so violently that there was no need for quiet.

No one would waste pity on a tiger if they had seen it kill. One trick with a victim that shows fight is to spring from behind and hamstring it, making it helpless and, without waiting to kill, begin eating. The tiger tried this with the little bull, but the bull would not be hamstrung. He fought for his life and the tiger had actually to give up this attack and go for the neck. Horatius' neck was solid, swelling muscle; he fought with all his strength and at that moment Dick shot the tiger.

In the light of the torch it lay, its head back on the

grass, the white of its stomach curiously lean, one enormous paw in the air, while the sound of the shot seemed to go on and on through the jungle. The tiger did not move again, though Dick threw stones at it from the knapsack, and he let off another two shots, close together, the signal for the elephants to come.

Bata Scully came slowly and for two or three hours Horatius had to stay, tied by the dead tiger, pawing at the ground like a bull in the bull ring, blood running from his wounds. The kill is usually finished off with a shot but—"He is standing up," said Dick. "He fought for his life and he shall have it." And we named him Horatius.

He was brought into camp and tied by a rope to a tree. If anyone came near him he fought, nearly breaking his neck with the rope, but when he realized that we meant to help his wounds, he was suddenly quiet and stood still, trembling, but not moving though he snorted through his nose. It was not pleasant for any of us; he was caked with blood and dung, and when that was washed off with water and permanganate, the wounds were terrible: claw slashes down his flanks, deep teeth marks in the thigh, and deeper holes each side of the neck.

"It will go septic," Neil warned us, "and what have you to put on it? You are not to take the only iodine. What can you use?"

What? If only there had been some tar, acriflavine,

anything. There was nothing but hot saline for fomentations and lanolin to block the holes and keep off the flies. It was pitifully inadequate but Nancy and I toiled, and the swelling began to go down. Horatius spent the days tied under the tree, a heap of grass beside him, and one bath towel tied round his neck to keep off the flies, another draped from his rump to his knee.

I could not leave the camp for long while he was so ill and I took to accompanying Mooltiki when she went wood-gathering or to fetch elephant food. It was always perilous to go out with her. A good elephant—Bata Scully, for instance—takes care of passengers, looking up when the mahout tells her, to see if they will escape being hit by an overhanging branch; if it seems doubtful her trunk will reach up and measure, then perhaps break off the branch. Mooltiki did not care if her whole load was swept away. Bata Scully would test a doubtful piece of ground carefully with her forefoot before putting her weight on it, while Mooltiki never looked where she was going and was quite likely to try to step into a quicksand or a bog, nor did she walk with the even pad-pad of most elephants; she had only two paces, scurry or dawdle, and if she lost her temper, which she frequently did, she was not above trying to shake us off with violent shruggings; but I could forgive her even this for the way she would fall, as I did, into a jungle dream and daze, forgetting what she had come out for, dawdling along, just looking.

There was so much to see and one never knew when one might see it: a porcupine; peacocks roosting in a low tree, their tail feathers folded and sweeping the ground; a single peacock, its crest and neck jewel green and blue; a florican; perhaps a python; monkeys. As soon as they saw us the monkeys dropped off the trees and ran. I had always thought it was the other way round, that they took to the trees and went away, swinging and leaping on the creepers. They were good-looking monkeys, deep pollen-yellow with long white tails and bluish faces, but they fled from us at sight, clutching their babies. We heard them chattering long after we had lost them in the jungle. More attractive were the cheetal, small deer with slender-boned legs and red coats spotted with white. They let us walk almost up to them on the elephant before they cantered away, hardly crackling a leaf and lifting neat little pairs of hoofs as they jumped over logs with a flick of their tails. There were hog deer, fatter, without spots, and everywhere there were butterflies: yellow ones, blue and white, dusty little black ones, and gorgeous swallowtails. All round the camp were pied kingfishers and jays, with heavenly blue in their wings and hideous quarrelsome voices.

We would wander and look, quite lost until the mahout would shout, equally startling Mooltiki and me. I would sit straighter and she would angrily begin picking up wood again.

Horatius was not improving. It was the flies; they were in a perpetual swarm around him; they would eat off the lanolin and crawl into the wounds. Now the leg, from haunch to hoof, was bloated and swollen. "I am afraid he will not do," said Neil.

Horatius was looking at us with his big, still calflike eyes, and, "Wait a little while," said Nancy. We boiled whole loaves of bread into a vast bread poultice and tied it on the wounds with dusters. Horatius appeared to like it very much.

After two days of making loaves and boiling them, the cook said he had run out of flour. No flour could be had nearer than the railhead until the lorry came at the end of the week. There was consternation until Bangla remembered that a market was held once every month in a village upstream, and that this was its day. "But that is Bhutan," said Nancy. "We haven't a permit."

Bangla smiled. "The Memsahib shall go with the cook," said Bangla, pointing at me. "They shall go for a ride. They do not want to cross the border but . . . Mooltiki is disobedient." That seemed likely enough even to satisfy Neil, and we went.

The village was on the edge of the river, twenty or thirty huts of matting and bamboo poles. A tame elephant seemed to be a curiosity and, as we came nearer, girls on their way to market threw themselves screaming off the path into the bushes, then sat up, their vegetables and chickens scattered round them, while they viewed this phenomenon of an elephant with a pad on its back, people sitting at ease—well, almost at ease—on top of it, and a little man astride the neck, driving by sticking his toes into the ears and prodding with a steel hook. Mooltiki entered the village at the head of a procession.

The market had not any stalls; it was held, simply, on the ground, and everyone left it to look at her. After she had let us get down, amid cries of admiration, she stood swaying in the middle of the only open space, where she looked almost as big as Bata Scully. It was Mooltiki's day; we were left to wander alone while she was offered sugar cane, banana leaves, and even oranges. Oranges were rare and expensive.

I walked between cloths spread with eggs, a few vegetables, bowls of roots and pulses, spice, celluloid combs and hairpins. There did not seem to be anything else except a wooden stand that displayed second-hand bottles and another with bales of cheap printed cotton and a case of gaudy beads. There were no animals, except a profusion of chickens and a small black kid curled in the dust. Every seller had the same few, cheap, common things, and in the middle a Marwari trader sat over a dirty piece of oilcloth marked with chequers and colours; when the men drifted back he gently cheated them out of most of the money they had. It was surprising what big stakes they put down, whole rupees, even five rupees.

The men were all dressed the same, in dun-white cotton breeches, black caps and waistcoats; the women nearly the same, in printed cotton skirts and bodices and coloured head-veils. The children were little replicas of their fathers and mothers, while the babies were naked. The village was the terminus of a dusty, thick-rutted road; everything was covered in dust and it all looked civilized, squalid, unappetizing. A little depressed, I went into one of the teashops; even the teashops were all the same, with a bench for customers, a platform of clay at one end topped with mats for sleeping, and a clay oven built in its side; above the oven, tea bowls were kept warm on a clay shelf.

I sat on the bench, watching the sleepy, desultory marketing going on. The cook went in search of the necessary flour and, as he was here, chickens, eggs, and some fresh vegetables as well, while Mooltiki still swayed from foot to foot, majestically eating her banana leaves. Then, from a jungle path along the road, a caravan came in and I knew there were still wild people, original, untouched by the world.

The porters were more like animals than men. They had short, brutish bodies, thick calves to their legs, faces that were flat, cheerful, and healthy-looking but quite uncomprehending. Their cheeks were red and

their slit eyes were bright, reflecting everything they
saw like a monkey's; they had huge fuzzes of hair
gummed stiff with dirt and vermin. Their clothes,
which had once been loose woollen robes, had become
pelts, a veneer of the original stuff lined thick with
their own grease and lice. As soon as they had put
down their packs, they went straight to the bead man.
It was not until they had been in the village for nearly
half an hour that they saw the elephant, when they
left the market in a tumult, running into the jungle
and coming out on hands and knees, or hiding behind
trees, clutching at each other.

With them were a chieftain and a woman. They
came to the teashop; he was as fat as Henry VIII and
had that king's haleness, a flat, fat, stupid, merry face,
and a beautiful skin with a bloom like a fruit. He was
dressed in grey, an inner and outer robe, and his hair
was cut on his shoulders with a fringe under a crown
of folded banana leaves.

She might have been his mother or his wife and it
was obvious at once that she was a personage. She was
little, merry too but with a comprehending merriness,
her eyes a clear amber brown set in wrinkles. Her hair
was cropped and she had small ears, flat to her head,
with square silver earrings. Her mouth was small and
her teeth like a child's, small and even, though she had
been eating betel and they were stained poppy red.
She was dressed in a blue robe with a dark red lining,

blue sleeves, and the striped apron of the Bhutanese married woman.

She sat down on the bench by me. The husband stood and stared at this apparition with a white skin but she courteously did not look but made quick little remarks, probably about the market and the weather, to the teashop hostess.

Presently I said in English, "May I look at your earrings?" and touched them lightly.

The earrings would not come off, though they were shown willingly. Then I handed across my dark glasses. Through the hostess the little queen asked, "How much?" and I said with my hands, "Nothing."

The hostess wore a silver ring. I touched that and asked, "How much?"

"Eight annas," said the hostess at once.

The ring was native silver and cut with charms. When the people saw that I had bought it they crowded round the teashop offering theirs until Henry VIII got up and contemptuously drove them away. We drank tea and he called for betel leaves and, when they were brought, started to roll them.

It was then that his wife took from the pouch of her robe the small box; it was for holding the paste that flavoured the leaves, a pleasing little box made of the same native silver but finer, chased with flowers and a pattern of clouds, the lid and bottom joined by a chain. She saw my eyes on it, and when she had

142

given Henry VIII some paste she put it into my hand.

"How much?"

For answer she took my other hand, pressed it over the box, and shook her head.

When we—the cook, his marketing, which now included a whole crate of live chickens, the mahout, Mooltiki, and I—left, the woman stood on the cliff, waving, waving. I still have the box but I never saw her again nor do I know who she was.

On the way back Mooltiki suffered from swelled head. She decided she could not bear the crate of live chickens on her back and beat at them with her trunk. The mahout screamed, we screamed, the chickens did their equivalent of screaming, but Mooltiki still slewed round. I thought she would knock us into the water but at that moment she stepped into a rapid. The water was milkily blue, running fast, and just as a child in a rage stops in mid-sob and, with tears on its cheeks, smiles, the little elephant, reduced now to her proper size, forgot the chickens and plunged her trunk into the eddies, blowing a cascade of bubbles.

As my time in the camp began to run out we were increasingly sad about Horatius. Loaf after loaf was boiled down but now the heap of grass, fresh every day, was carried away untouched and the little bull's eyes had a heavy glaze. There was even pus on his eyelids and, "I had better put a shot into him," said Neil but, "Wait," said Bangla, and I pleaded, "Wait."

On my last day but one Dick wounded a tiger that retreated into a stretch of high grass on the edge of a narrow arm of the river. An elephant was needed to get it out, but Secunda had gone with Neil on a tour of inspection, while Bata Scully had stomach trouble— an elephant with stomach trouble is an impressive sight. Mooltiki of course was ruled out for such dangerous work, yet the wounded tiger could not be left alive. Wounded, it might begin to take cattle and even men, for that is how man-eaters are made, but how was Dick to get it? He said, "I shall go to the opposite side of the river, lie up there, and wait till it comes down in the evening to drink, and shoot it across the water."

"It could be like that," said Bangla.

Dick said that the mahout must take Mooltiki round behind the stretch of grass and wait. "When I shout across, she can go in," said Dick. The mahout demurred. "She is not afraid of a dead tiger, is she?" asked Dick.

"She must not be," said Bangla, which closed the matter and, towards four o'clock, Mooltiki set out. Against my better judgment, I went with her.

"I shouldn't stay on her if I were you," said Dick. "Make her put you up a tree."

Mooltiki, with the mahout and me, walked round the back of the grass; we had only a *kukhri*, the native wide-bladed knife, between us, and it seemed to me we took a long time to find a suitable tree. "What if the tiger comes out while we are near?" I had asked Dick.

"Why should it? It won't disturb itself for an elephant."

"A tame elephant with people on its back?"

"It won't know you are on its back if you don't talk," said Dick witheringly.

The tree was bare and leafless. Mooltiki walked under the lowest branch; she had sensed that something was in the grass and it was very unwillingly that she halted to let me climb up. Standing upright on the back of a swaying elephant is difficult, particularly when one knows a wounded tiger is not far away; Mooltiki made it more difficult still. She sidled and fidgeted and, when the mahout took his attention off her for a moment to help me, she walked off. I was left hanging by my arms.

I looked down at the bald, dusty path below, singularly bald and exposed; I looked at the sinister grass. My arms felt as if they were cracking. There was no Bangla to help me this time, but terror can make one do superhuman—or subhuman—things, and I managed to wriggle myself nearer the trunk and, with my feet braced against it, in an undignified monkey fashion, climb up, though a dizzy blackness filled my eyes. After a while I felt pleased with myself. I had managed to get up and not cry out, which might have startled the tiger away.

The tree was a respectable height and overhung both grass and river. Mooltiki had disappeared and presently I saw Dick and Bangla creep into position on the opposite bank.

It was again that jungle quiet, so quiet that the river seemed to run loudly between its stones. The sun was disappearing behind the trees, there was no sunlight in the thickets of grass, only on the water where a shaft of sun lay. Then in the river three little otters began to play. They swam in quick circles after each other, only their heads, whiskers, and teeth showing above the water with long ripples to mark the steering of their tails, which they used as rudders. When they came to the shallows the whole of them showed, small and exceedingly glossy, their fur almost oily with wetness; they bounced half in, half out of the water, splashing each other as people do on the beach. All at once they reared themselves back in a row and stared, and I looked down and saw the tiger.

Distracted by the otters, I had not sensed him before. At first he was only a darkness in the grass, then slowly, very slowly, he put out a foot. I—and the otters, I thought—held our breath as he pulled himself slowly after the foot. He was long and lean, a length of stripes, his shoulders hunched and his white undercoat touching the grass. He seemed suspicious and very angry; his tail moved in jerks like that of an angry cat and he looked up and down the river. When his face turned towards me, it looked large for the rest of him, wide between the ears, almost swollen in the cheeks, touched with white. The otters slipped into the water and reared themselves up farther away to stare again while I sat so still that my bones seemed set. On the other bank a sunspot gleamed and disappeared again as the barrel of the rifle came up.

The moment settled into a long suspicious stillness. It seemed impossible that the tiger should be taken in with the quiet sky and the brooding trees, the still grass on the opposite bank, the river's cool water, and the otters, though they were harmlessly tumbling again, the water drops from their whiskers flashing in that shaft of sun. The tiger lowered his head and I heard a sound I heard from my dogs in my own house every day, the lapping of water in loud, thirsty laps.

The tiger lapped and then, with a shock, the rifle fired from the other bank. It was a long shot and it missed. He crouched, water dripping off his cheeks, snarled, and slowly retreated backwards into the grass. I heard him moving away with a slithering, rustling movement in the grass.

He was wounded and very thirsty; he did not go far and soon, surprisingly quickly, he came back to drink again, this time in a muddy inlet farther off.

There the grass stopped short of the water by several feet and I saw him clearly, crouched down in his exciting shape above the river. I had him in my field-glasses and nothing was hidden, from the pale linings of his ears to the angry tip of his tail; along his side the beautiful striped markings rippled into each other as he moved. He drank, lifted his head, and the rifle fired again.

His death was so much in the tradition of tiger deaths that I could not believe I had seen it. He gave a roar that sent echoes flying over the river to the hills, reared up like a tiger on a crest, and fell backwards; one paw beat and swooped, then he lay still.

I sat in my tree, and presently realized that I was very stiff. On the opposite bank Dick was stretching himself, and Bangla, his hands round his mouth, was hallooing to Mooltiki to come and fetch them. While the sun went down, Mooltiki waded across and came back, carrying them and grumbling and flapping her ears.

The mahout turned her to the inlet and she walked along, petulantly thumping and smacking her trunk in the grass, not looking where she was going until all at once she saw the tiger; her trunk came up and her trumpet was such an agonized squeal that Bata Scully heard and answered from the elephant lines. Mooltiki shied, but her mahout stabbed her so passionately on the forehead that at last she went in closer and Bangla was able to stand up on her pad and throw stones at the tiger; then, very cautiously and ungraciously, Mooltiki let him slide off into the grass and, covered by

Dick, go to look. In a moment Bangla's thumb came up. The tiger was dead.

Bangla whistled and after a time, round the grass, came the rest of the *shikaris* and most of the camp. They roped the tiger's paws and, all together heaving, using the rope as a pulley, they hoisted the tiger onto Mooltiki's back in spite of her fuss and fury. Bangla always treated Mooltiki as if her feelings and the impressive way she showed them were childish gambols or a little woman's whims. Then Mooltiki, with the tiger riding high, came to fetch me.

I wished Bangla had come. It was nearly dark and I did not like it any more than Mooltiki. All the way home she trumpeted, rounding on herself with an angry trunk, shrugging, making the mahout cry out, a feeble little noise after hers. The tiger head lolled and bumped and blood came trickling out of its mouth while its paws went gradually stiff. The immensity of those paws was a surprise, great, sinewy lengths with pads under them like the rollers on skates, and now I saw that its coat, which had looked so velvety in the distance, was bristly and scarred and full of ticks sucking themselves fat and loathsome on blood. I wished that I and it could have gone home separately.

"You must see the skinning," said Dick, and, when I shuddered, "It isn't disgusting, it's so perfectly done." It was not even bloody. The sharp knives slipped between the skin and the tissues so that it was more like an undressing than a skinning. Tail and legs were slit down the seam—or where the seam should have been—and the paws with their claws were peeled off inside out as one would remove a glove. The mask was taken off neatly round the jaws and eyes and the tiger was left, naked and gleaming, with strappings of white and red muscles and cobweb-white tissues.

The skin was cleaned of its ticks and lice, pegged out under the shade of the hut, and rubbed with wood ash and salt; a collection of tiger chops went to the cookhouse for the servants' supper and before dawn next morning a silent procession moved through the camp, people come from the villages to get the rare and fresh meat. They carried it away on their backs or heads, or fastened a haunch to a pole between two men. Then the carcass was left to the vultures. They had appeared out of an empty sky and the trees were full of them, birds like rocs, with horrible sinister faces. In a few hours they had eaten all that was left.

Next morning when I came to dress Horatius' wounds a piece of flesh fell off into my hand and it was alive with maggots. They were in every hole and I cried out, sick and horrified. Bangla came hurrying up. "Look! Look!" I said, almost crying, but he smiled.

"Now he will get better," said Bangla, and that night when I went to see the little bull, thinking of his pain, of how he was unable to lie down and would be visited by terrors, made worse by the smell of the second tiger, Horatius was lying down and his small, humped shape looked comfortable.*

He was safe between the campfire and the *shikaris*. The fires burned high, the sparks flying up, as they always did, against the stars. The cold snow wind was blowing and, satisfied, I turned towards warmth, dinner, and whisky. Then, on the river bed, I saw a familiar small blur, Mooltiki working late. She came loaded across the river and I stayed to watch her climb wearily out of the water for the last time.

She went to the elephant lines, the tired mahout took off the load, loosened the ropes, and dropped the pad. He fastened Mooltiki's leg chains and spread an inviting meal of leaves, cane, and *dhan*, a kind of grain. Squatting beside her, he wrapped the grain in banana leaves, making envelopes which he posted in her mouth. Sometimes he spread the grain on a cloth, letting her pick it up for herself with her trunk, which she would do to the last, last grain, but tonight she was too hungry for that; using not both hands but her trunk, she stuffed leaves in, alternately with the mahout's envelopes. She looked a happy, relaxed little elephant at last, but the life of a tweeny is hard.

The sparks in the fire had died down and Neil clapped his hands.

---

* *He recovered completely and went back to his village to become the leader of the herd.*